Gary dropped me into the ocean with a splash. It was freezing! I screamed and stood up, then sputtered, "I'll get you." But he was already running down the sand, laughing over his shoulder.

I took after him. I'm a fast runner, but I wouldn't have caught him if he hadn't stumbled over a pile of seaweed. I grabbed his arm, and we fell in a jumbled heap in the surf.

The tide was just going out, and as the sand slid from underneath us, we grabbed at each other to keep from being pulled with it. I was suddenly very conscious of the odd mixture of cold water and Gary's warm arms, which were still wrapped around me. When I looked up, all I could see was his face. His eyes were very green.

Then I remembered the pink letters doused in perfume that he'd gotten from California. "I—I think we'd better start looking for shells," I said.

Don't Forget Me

Diana Gregory

BANTAM BOOKS
TORONTO · NEW YORK · LONDON · SYDNEY · AUCKLAND

RL 5, IL age 11 and up

DON'T FORGET ME
A Bantam Book / December 1984

*Sweet Dreams and its associated logo
are registered trademarks of Bantam Books, Inc.
Registered in U.S. Patent and Trademark Office and elsewhere.*

Cover photo by Pat Hill

ISBN 0-553-24381-0

Published simultaneously in the United States and Canada

---

*Bantam Books are published by Bantam Books, Inc. Its trademark,
consisting of the words "Bantam Books" and the portrayal of a
rooster, is registered in U.S. Patent and Trademark Office and in
other countries. Marca Registrada. Bantam Books, Inc., 666 Fifth
Avenue, New York, New York 10103.*

Printed and bound in Great Britain by Hunt Barnard Printing Ltd.

O   0 9 8 7 6 5 4 3 2 1

Don't Forget Me

Chapter One

I pretended not to notice as Stephanie Henderson broke off from the group she was with and headed across the street in my direction. She was waving in that exaggerated way she liked to affect. "Yoo-hoo—Wendy! Wendy Ferris—wait up a second. I want to ask you something—something I heard this afternoon."

I tried not to act as if I were ignoring her— even though that's exactly what I wanted to do. I knew she just wanted new gossip, and I wasn't the slightest bit interested in supplying her with any. But considering how effective she was at nosing out any new happenings, I knew it wouldn't be long before she, and everyone else, knew everything—or worse. Stephanie liked to take facts and twist them around to suit her own purposes. Sometimes I thought Stephanie was just biding time in school until she could apply for a permanent position as a reporter for one of those horrible weekly scandal sheets.

Trying to look casual, I shifted my book

pack onto one shoulder and turned down the path leading across the empty lot toward the beach. I hurried. If Stephanie wanted to catch up to me, she'd have to chase through the sea oats and sandburs to do it. And I honestly didn't think she'd want to, not in the high-heeled sandals she was wearing.

I was right; it worked. I glanced nonchalantly over my left shoulder to see that Stephanie had stopped on the edge of the sidewalk before walking back to join the other kids.

Once safely out of sight, I changed my mind about going right home. I decided to double back and take the long way through the business section of town, thinking I'd do some window-shopping, maybe stop in at the Dune Diner for a Coke or something. Anything to put off having to go home.

Home. Big laugh that was. Home was now the guest bedroom at my Aunt Eva's.

That was probably what Stephanie wanted to ask me about. Not that my personal tragedy was any huge secret. But it was still new, and I hurt too much to answer a lot of questions from someone like Stephanie Henderson, champion of school gossip.

Wendy, I told myself, as I walked toward the main boulevard, *you've got to stop being so gloomy. It's too nice a day for ugly thoughts.*

And it was. It was still early in the

afternoon—our school was on a double schedule, and the seniors and juniors, like me, got the early session. The sun was warm on my shoulders, and my pink tank top and wraparound denim skirt looked perfect for the sunny day. As the Gulf breeze blew my hair away from my face, I took a deep breath, enjoying the wonderful, tangy smell of the ocean.

I loved living in Florida, especially near the Gulf. I'd lived in Sea Gate all my life, and I simply couldn't imagine living anywhere else.

Turning onto the main street, I passed the drugstore, which was about as old-fashioned a drugstore as could be found. It even had a movie-set soda counter, which dispensed superthick, giant malts.

My first stop was the reduced-book table by the front door of the Sandcastle Book Nook. I was big on bargain books—almost addicted. I paused and picked up a book with a photo of a cowrie shell on the cover. Shells were a great love of mine.

But soon after flipping through the book, I realized it wasn't for me. It was more for beginners. I put it back and picked up a mystery, looking at the last page to see how it ended before putting it back, too. I'd never buy a mystery unless I liked the ending. I waved at the owner, Mrs. Goodson, and she waved back. She was really sweet and would sometimes save books for me that she thought I'd like. I really wasn't ready to spend any money on books that day, though. I was saving for something special.

That something special was next door in the Breeze-In Sportswear Shop. For the past week there had been this absolutely fantastically sexy, green, one-piece bathing suit in the window. I only needed a few more dollars in order to pay for it.

I walked down the sidewalk until I was right in front of the window. Then I turned and let out a sigh of relief. The suit was still there, draped artistically next to a plastic palm tree.

But as I was looking at the suit, picturing myself wearing it, a hand reached into the window and lifted it out.

For a second I couldn't believe it. I frowned, then told myself there had to be some explanation. Maybe they were changing the display. After all, the suit had been there all week. Or maybe someone had decided the suit should be put back on the rack before it got faded from being in the window too long.

I had to go inside and find out for sure.

After the bright sunlight outside, it seemed dark in the store, and blinking, I turned toward the nearest rack. Then I started pushing through some tops, even though I still couldn't see anything.

"Dear," this high, nasal voice said right in my ear, making me jump about a foot, "I don't think you really want one of those. Those are maternity tops."

"Oh—oh." I looked up into the face of a middle-aged woman wearing a ton of bright blue eye shadow. "Actually I wasn't looking for a top. I was looking for a bathing suit." I felt totally dumb.

"Well, in that case, dear, why are you looking on this rack? Why don't you look on the rack where the bathing suits are hanging?" She pointed with a long, orange-painted fingernail at a circular rack three feet away. "They're right there."

"Oh—ah, thank you." I walked over and began looking through my size, then through the sizes on either side of mine, but my suit wasn't there. I started to panic. Then I saw it, way at the back of the store. A saleslady was just handing it through the closed curtains of a dressing room. I watched as the suit disappeared from sight.

I moved closer and stood there, glaring at the closed curtains. When the curtains parted, a girl about my age, fifteen or sixteen, stuck her head out. She looked right at me. It was one of those embarrassing moments when you're caught staring. I flashed her a quick smile and tried to appear casual.

She just smiled back in a friendly way. "Hey, do you see a mirror out there? I can't tell very much from the one in here. No," she said, shaking her head. "What I mean is I don't really want to look at myself in it. It makes me look positively humungus."

The smile I gave back was real this time. "I know exactly what you mean. Dressing-room mirrors make me want to diet for a year." I nodded toward the side of the store. "There's a pretty good one over there. And, if you go around behind those racks, no one from the street can see you."

"Hey, thanks," she said, stepping out. And when I saw her, my heart fell to the bottom of my stomach. She looked great in the suit.

I watched as she made her way through the crowd of filled clothing racks to the three-sided mirror. She turned shyly in front of it, biting her lip in concentration.

Funny, when I'd first spotted the suit in the window, I'd decided the color was perfect for me. I had a great tan since I practically lived on the beach all year. My hair was brown, and my eyes were the same color green as the suit.

This girl didn't look at all like me, but the suit was dynamite on her. I knew she couldn't be from Florida because her skin was creamy ivory. Her dark brown hair fell smoothly almost to her waist; she made me wish my hair wasn't short. I hated saying it, but I couldn't help myself. "It looks great!"

"Really?" She stuck her hands on her hips. "You really think so?"

"Boy, I should look so terrific in a suit."

"Oh, come on," she said, cocking her head and looking at me, "you have a great fig—"

She was interrupted by an older woman with identical coloring, who walked over to join her at the mirror. I decided that she had to be the girl's mother and that she did not share my opinion of the suit.

The woman frowned, then reached out and tugged at the leg of the suit. "I don't know, darling. Do you really think it's right for you? I do think it's cut rather high."

Just then the saleslady sailed up, wearing this big saleslady-type smile. "Oh, but that's the way all the teenage girls are wearing them." She touched the girl's shoulder, making her pivot to show off the suit. "And aren't they the lucky ones? Don't you wish we could wear something as lovely?"

The girl shot me a quick look and smiled. I grinned back. We both knew she was going to end up owning the suit.

I'd wanted that suit very much. But as I left the store, I realized I was glad the other girl was getting it. She was nice, and I really liked her.

Speaking to her reminded me of how lonely I'd been all week, purposefully avoiding my friends and barely speaking to my best friend, Marlo Williams. If I didn't do something to change soon, I'd end up a hermit crab.

Chapter Two

Aunt Eva's house was at the end of Pelican Lane. It was pink with a large, old bougainvillea vine planted near the front door. The shiny, dark-green leaves and bright scarlet flowers spilled onto the roof. It was a pretty house. The only problem was that I didn't feel as if I belonged in it.

Using the brand-new key Aunt Eva had had made for me, I let myself in. Inside it was cool, the drapes pulled to keep out the sun. I closed the door and let my bookpack drop to the floor next to a fragile-looking antique table in the entry hall. "Aunt Eva," I called. "I'm here."

"I'm out in the Florida room, Wendy," her voice came floating through the house. "Come join me."

I went through the living room to the glassed-in porch where Aunt Eva sat curled up on a wicker chaise that was piled with green-and-white print cushions.

"Hi, love," she said, smiling brightly at

8

me. "Want some iced tea?" She had been trying hard all week to make me feel welcome, but it wasn't working. I smiled weakly and slid into the fan-backed chair opposite the chaise.

"I just got home myself a little while ago," she went on, leaning over the small table to pour tea. "I have had a day you wouldn't believe!" She added a slice of lemon and handed the glass to me. "I showed that old white elephant of a house, the one I told you about on Castle, to six different parties. And, would you believe it, one of the couples liked it but didn't make an offer because it doesn't have a dishwasher!"

She picked up her own glass and took a sip. "Here they were, ready to spend thousands and thousands of dollars for a house, and they weren't willing to spend a couple hundred to put in a dishwasher. There are times when I wonder why I ever decided to go into real estate."

She studied me for a moment over the rim of her glass. "So, tell me, how was school today?"

"OK," I shrugged. Then, feeling guilty, I tried to make conversation. "We had this pop quiz in history. I don't think I did very well."

She nodded. "Umm, I used to hate pop quizzes, too. I never thought they were very fair."

"Right." I nodded back, then tried to think of what to say next. I drank more tea.

Aunt Eva glanced away pretending to be concerned about a perfectly healthy plant.

It was strange. I was much more like her than my own mother. Both of us had short brown hair, only Aunt Eva's was curly, and short all over, while mine was cut short on the sides but was longer in the back.

Mom's hair was brown, too, but a honey brown. Her nose was perfect, not too short like mine. Sometimes my eyes looked like hers, but only in shape because hers were deep, almost violet, blue.

When I was very little, I used to wait for the magic moment when I would wake up some morning and look like Mom. One day I asked my father when that was going to happen. He took me on his lap and told me, "Wendy, you are one of a kind. You are never going to look like anyone but yourself. And you're lucky, too, because," he said, stopping to kiss my nose, "you have fairy dust right there." He meant my freckles, which are hard to see unless you look very, very close. Then he smiled. "You didn't know that, did you?" And we both laughed as he hugged me very tight.

Thinking about that time made my eyes begin to burn. I still missed my father very much, even though it had been a long time since he'd died.

I put the glass on the tray and started to

get up. "I think I'll go change into something else, I'm kind of hot from walking home."

"Sure, honey. By the way, something came in the mail for you."

Aunt Eva picked up a long, white envelope that I hadn't noticed before and held it out. When I saw the address written on the front, I didn't take it. Instead, I sat back down on the edge of the chair and stared at it. The letter was from my mother. I'd been expecting it.

"Well," Aunt Eva said, giving a small shrug, "you don't have to read it right this minute." She laid the letter on the table where I could reach it. "But perhaps you'd like to take it with you. You could always read it later."

Nodding slightly, I picked up the letter, then let it drop into my lap.

Aunt Eva pretended not to notice how I was acting. "Your mother wrote to me, too." She smiled. "She's found a nice apartment that isn't too far from her job. From the way she writes, good apartments are hard to find. I guess she was lucky." Eva gave me another brief smile. "She misses you."

"Uh-huh," I heard myself say. That part I didn't believe one bit. If she missed me so much, then what was she doing with a new apartment a thousand miles away in a strange city? Why wasn't she still living in Florida with me? "Excuse me," I said, standing up. "I think

I'll go change now." I glanced at Aunt Eva and saw a brief, unhappy expression in her eyes.

"Umm—is there anything you'd like me to do for you this afternoon? Any errands, anything?"

She shook her head. "No, Wendy. You just go do whatever it is you'd like to do."

I nodded, picked up the letter, and left the room. In the entry I picked up my book bag and went down the hall to the guest room.

Chapter Three

I tossed the letter onto the top of the dresser, kicked off my espadrilles, and threw myself down on the bed, burying my face in the pink, quilted satin comforter.

After a few minutes I sat up cross-legged and looked around the room. Pale blue carpet. Pink and blue daisy wallpaper. French provincial furniture—blond wood instead of the usual white. Pale blue dust ruffle under the pink satin comforter on the bed. Pale blue organdy curtains at the windows. It was a beautiful room all right, but I didn't want to live in it.

"It's all your fault," I said aloud, glaring at the letter. "Why can't you be like other mothers? I hate you!" For a moment I felt really horrible about saying that. But then I remembered what had happened only a week before. . . .

I'd come home to find Mom still in the apartment. That surprised me because usually she'd already left for work by the time I got home from school. I heard her doing something in her bedroom, and I went to investigate. She was packing. She was standing in front of an open suitcase on the bed, with a bunch of panty hose in one hand and a slip with a broken strap that was hanging down in the other.

"Hi, uh, Mom." I frowned. "What are you doing?"

"Oh, Wendy." She glanced up, startled. "Aren't you home early? What time is it, anyway?"

"No," I answered. "I'm home at the right time. But why aren't you at work? And what are you packing for?"

"Uh . . ." She scowled but didn't say anything. It was as if she were searching hard for the right words. Then she just sat down on the edge of the bed next to the suitcase. "Wendy—" She looked up. "Wendy, you know what?" Her blue eyes turned really violet. "I've been offered a real job." She went on in this excited voice. "It's with one of the best cosmetic companies around."

Then, all at once, she began carefully folding the slip so I couldn't see her eyes. "It means I have to leave by the end of this week."

"You mean you have to go on a business trip?" I asked. "To meet with someone about the job?"

"No—no." She arranged the slip. "The job is in Philadelphia."

14

"Philadelphia?"

"Yes." She shot the word out.

My mind was whirling. Philadelphia was up north. Up north was cold. It was a place visitors came to Florida to get away from. Therefore, it had to be a miserable place. "Mom, I don't want to move to Philadelphia," I insisted. "I'd hate it there."

Mom carefully folded the slip and put it in the suitcase before answering me. "Wendy," she said, finally looking at me. Her eyes were glittery; she was either angry or about to cry. "Wendy, I've already considered that you would feel exactly that way. And that's why I've decided it would be best if you stayed here. In Florida."

"Here!" I stared at her. "You mean you're going to leave me here? Alone?"

"Oh, no—no, of course not. Not alone. You're going to live with your aunt Eva."

"But I don't want to live with Aunt Eva!" I insisted. "I want to live with you." I took a step toward her. "Why do you have to take this stupid job, anyway? Why don't you just tell them you don't want the job?"

"Wendy, please—we've talked about this before. You know I've hoped for just this kind of career offer for a long time. I don't intend to be stuck behind a drugstore counter for the rest of my life. Why do you think I went back to school and got my degree after your father died—and worked evenings so I could do it?"

She leaned toward me, the knuckles of both hands white. "Wendy, tell me, what do *you* want for me?"

"If it's the money," I said, thinking I was being very reasonable, "I'll get a job after school. Other kids have jobs."

"Wendy, understand—" Her voice was tight. "It isn't the money. Wendy, please." She shook her head. Then she stood up. "Everything is already settled. Eva said she would be happy to have you stay with her. I thought about bringing you to Philadelphia, but I decided you probably wouldn't be happy there. And I'll be working long hours—"

"Oh, that's it—that's it! Isn't it?" I heard my voice rising to a shriek. "That's what this is all about, a precious job. All you can think about is a career. You don't really care about me, do you? No, no, I'm just something to get rid of—like furniture. What *are* you going to do about the furniture, by the way?" I was practically screaming. "Are you going to dump *that* on Aunt Eva, too?"

"No, Wendy." Mom's voice was so low I could barely hear it. "I'm putting the furniture into storage."

"Oh, terrific, terrific. Well, why don't you just put me in storage, too?" I screamed.

"Wendy, please—let's talk."

"Oh, forget it," I spat out. "Just forget it." Then I stormed into the bathroom and slammed the door.

A few minutes later there was a soft knock on the door. "Wendy, please understand." The knock was repeated. "This job is such a marvelous opportunity—"

"Go away!" I yelled. "I'm not listening. I'm putting my hands over my ears."

I stayed in the bathroom for a long time, sitting on the floor, my back against the side of the cold tub. I was crammed so full of conflicting emotions that I didn't know which one to concentrate on first. I started out being angry and ground my teeth so hard they hurt. Then feeling horribly sorry for myself, I cried. Then I got mad all over again and shredded an entire roll of toilet paper.

When I finally went out, I walked right past Mom's open door to my own room and shut my door. Once Mom came to tell me dinner was ready. I didn't answer her. Later she said she just wanted to talk for a few minutes. I didn't answer then, either. I could hear her standing quietly outside the door for a long time.

The next few days were terrible. When I wasn't in school, I spent most of my time in my room, packing and thinking about how my life had suddenly been turned upside down. Mom spent a lot of time packing, too. We hardly talked.

She left very early Saturday morning. We had said our goodbyes, if you could call it that, since I was barely speaking to Mom, the night before.

When I woke up, the apartment was quiet. My breakfast was on the table, and there was a note propped up against the glass of orange juice.

In it Mom wrote that she hoped someday I'd realize how she felt. She added that she loved me very much and would miss me terribly. I screwed up my face at that. Then she finished the note by saying that she would write a long, long letter to me as soon as she was settled in. . . .

Well, this must be the letter. I glanced at it again. But I didn't need to read it to know what was in it. In fact, I'd promised myself I'd never read it.

I was still sitting cross-legged on the bed when the phone started to ring a few minutes later. I waited until it had rung seven times before deciding Aunt Eva wasn't going to answer it. Then I ran into the hall to pick it up.

"Hello!"

"Wendy?" It was Marlo, my best friend. "Is that you? You sound funny. Hey, where the heck did you disappear to after school today? I looked all over for you."

"Oh—uh," I stuttered, trying to think of an excuse. "Sorry," I said. "I had to run an errand for my aunt—the market—"

"Uh-huh." Marlo's voice was disbelieving.

"Just like you've suddenly started having to run errands all week. Come off it, Wendy. Give me a break." I could just imagine her tossing her long, blond hair off her shoulders with a typical impatient gesture. "I know you just wanted to go off and mope some more." I heard her take a deep breath. "Now you listen to me, Wendy. You've been doing this for exactly one week, and I think it's time you stopped. Because if you don't, you're going to turn into some kind of pathetic mental case. And I won't stand for it. Do you hear me?"

"OK, OK," I said. "I give up. I promise I'll try to do better. Satisfied?"

"Absolutely not," she scolded. "You need real therapy. You have to get out and stop being so antisocial. You don't want people to really start talking about you, do you?" She didn't let me answer. "Now go get your suit on and meet me down by the path. And hurry up. Because I've got a surprise. There's someone I want you to meet."

"Oh, no, Marlo, please!" I groaned. "I'm definitely not in the mood to meet anyone. Who is it, some new guy?"

Marlo collected male admirers the way some people collect stamps.

"No, not exactly," she said, hedging. "But I'm not about to tell you over the phone. You'll just have to come out of your shell long enough to find out for yourself." She paused. "Well, are you coming?"

"Oh, I don't know." I leaned against the wall and stared at a framed print of a hibiscus flower. "Oh, all right. Give me five minutes to change."

"Five minutes," Marlo snapped. "No more." Then she hung up before I could change my mind.

Darn, I really wasn't in the mood to meet someone new. Still, the hot sun and the salty gulf breeze blowing through my hair might be the very things to bring me around.

Back in my room I started rummaging through the dresser drawers. In only a week I'd managed to turn them into my usual state of chaos. And, somehow, that made me feel just a little bit more at home. Finally I managed to locate two pieces of the same bathing suit.

A few minutes later I was standing in front of the mirror adjusting the halter top of my electric blue bikini. After adding some fresh lip gloss and running a brush over my hair, I was ready. I slipped into my beach thongs and went out to tell my aunt where I was going.

Chapter Four

Marlo's was one of the houses on the beach side of Gulf Highway. The path where we usually met ran between a couple of the houses down to the sand. Walking up the side of the highway, I could see her waiting for me near a clump of palms. I waved. She waved back. Then I noticed the girl standing beside her, and I almost couldn't believe it.

"Hi!" the girl in the green bathing suit said as I crossed the highway to them. Then she kind of giggled. "I guess it's a small world."

"Huh-uh." I shook my head and found myself laughing back. "It's just a small beach."

"Oh, right—right."

"Hey!" Marlo looked back and forth at the two of us. "Do you know each other from someplace else, or something?"

"Hmm, something," I said, nodding, then explained. "We met this afternoon at Breeze-In."

"And"—the girl stepped in front of us and

began pivoting like a fashion model—"she helped me pick out this suit. Don't you just love it? My mother positively hates it." Stopping, she put one hand behind her head and struck a pose. "She says it shows too much of the *real* me."

"Oh, but, daaaarling," Marlo said, throwing her head back and staring down her nose, "how else are you doing to get a tan that will simply devastate the boys?"

"Well, the tan never will be. I wear a sunscreen all the time—I really burn."

"Well," I said, realizing I really liked her, "the important thing is that you ended up with the suit."

"Absolutely!" she agreed.

"Hey!" I turned to Marlo. "We still don't know each other's names. Don't just stand there—introduce us."

"Listen," Marlo said defensively, "I figured if you two were on such buddy-buddy terms that she'd let you help her pick out a suit, you were probably on a first-name basis."

"Well." The girl smiled at me. "I could tell right away that she had excellent taste. Hi! I'm Samantha Vries."

"Hi!" I said, "I'm Wendy Ferris."

"Oh—and this is my brother, Gary."

My first impression of the person who stepped out from the shadows of the palms was that he was terrifically good-looking, a jogger who probably liked black olives on his pizza.

I got those kinds of instant impressions, like with the pizza thing. I usually found out later that I was right.

As for his being good-looking, that would have been obvious to anyone. He had the same kind of straight, even features Samantha had, but on him they were arranged just the way I thought they should be on a guy. Unlike Samantha, though, he had a tan. And his eyes were this incredible green, like sun shining through emeralds.

As for his being a jogger, that was easy. One jogger can always tell another one. Besides, he was wearing a cut-off sweat shirt and shorts that had those kind of creases only gotten from running and sweating at the same time.

"Hi!" I said, sticking out my hand and smiling my best smile.

"Hello," he said back. But it wasn't with any great enthusiasm. And, after he shook my hand, he did this combination frown and sigh, then put both hands on his hips and just stood there staring as if he were waiting for me to say some *dumb*, girl-type thing.

Well, of course what I did was to scowl back.

The big silence built up.

We could have stayed that way forever. Finally he moved. His face first, the frown

23

deepening. I noticed how it didn't go at all with the little laugh lines around his eyes.

"Excuse me," he said. "I've got to run."

And he really meant just that. Because he took off at a jog and headed down the sandy shoulder of the street.

"I don't believe it!" I said through my own scowl. "What did *I* do?"

"Oh, wow!" Samantha groaned. "Look, Wendy," she said, reaching over and putting her hand briefly on my arm, "I'm sorry about that. Let me apologize for Gary. He's normally not that rude. Usually he can be counted on to be a pretty decent sort of guy. It's just that he has some problems right now, and he's trying to work them out. He's not the greatest at covering up his feelings."

"Don't worry," I told Samantha. "I understand!"

I guess I must have sounded *too* understanding. Samantha looked at me in a very curious way. And Marlo shot me a warning look.

"Hey, all right, everybody," she said brightly to break the mood. "What are we doing standing here? Let's go where the action is." She pulled both of us toward the path to the beach.

"So, and just where is all the action?" Samantha wanted to know.

"I think we're headed for The Grass Hut," I told her.

"Correct." Marlo explained to Samantha, "The Grass Hut is where all the kids hang out at the beach. It looks like a real grass shack and has tables outside with thatched umbrellas. It's where we do most of our serious eating—and messing around."

We came out on the beach and kicked off our thongs, stuffing them under a nearby sea grape bush. As we walked along in the surf, I only half listened as Marlo tried to convince Samantha she should try a conch burger, Florida's answer to the standard American hamburger. Scuffing my feet through the softly curling foam, I let my mind wander. I thought about Samantha's brother, Gary, and wondered if his problems were as terrible as mine. I didn't think they could be. But if they were, I definitely could understand the reason why he'd acted the way he had when we'd been introduced. That was exactly the same way I'd been acting all week long. I bent down and picked up a broken whelk shell and skimmed it out across the waves.

"Hey, Wendy." Marlo tapped my shoulder. "Come back to planet Earth and tell Samantha how great conch burgers are. She won't believe me."

"Yuck!" I stuck my tongue out. "You should know better than to ask me to recommend those things to anyone." I turned to Samantha. "No, honest. I guess you should try them. I know it's strange, having grown up in

25

Florida, and all, but I don't like seafood—in any shape."

"Hmm, sorry, Marlo." Samantha shook her head. "I think I kind of agree with Wendy."

We walked along without saying anything for a while, and then Samantha blurted out, "You know, I think I'm going to like it here— just as long as I can continue to have regular hamburgers."

"Hey!" I said, turning to her. "Does that mean you're more than one of Marlo's family's guests? You're not just here for a couple of weeks?"

Marlo's family was very sociable, always having people visit from other parts of the country. Marlo's house was large, and her mother loved cooking for a crowd.

Marlo grinned. "I knew there was something important I forgot to tell you, Wendy. Samantha's my mysterious surprise. But some surprise. And when I found out you'd already met, I completely forgot about telling you she's here to stay. The Vrieses are just staying with us until they find a house to rent."

"Oh, hey, that's great!" I said and turned to Samantha.

"Well, great—if we get to stay." Samantha made a face. "I'm not holding my breath. See, my father is an engineer with Lambert Industries. And what that means is that just about the time we get settled into some place, my father gets notified that he's been transferred again. There are times when I don't think we should even bother to unpack."

"How tough," I said sympathetically.

"But, Samantha," Marlo insisted, "you said that wasn't going to happen this time. You said your father's been put in charge of a huge project that's going to take years to complete. Didn't you?"

"Yeah, right." Samantha nodded. "But ask me again in a year—if we're still here."

"Maybe this time really will be different," I ventured.

"Oh, I hope so."

Just then I spotted a perfect shell. Reaching down I picked it up and handed it to her. "Welcome to Florida," I said.

She held it in the flat of her hand. It was a lace murex, white and fragile-looking. "Oh, it's pretty." She smiled. "I'll consider it a good omen."

We started walking through the water again. "Is that why your brother's so angry? Because you've moved again?"

"Hmmm—that's part of it, but not all of it."

The way she looked, I was sorry I'd asked the question. I was about to tell her to forget it.

"You know, I probably shouldn't feel this way because I don't think what Gary's planning to do is right, but I can't really blame him." Samantha gave each of us a look. "Please don't tell anyone what I'm telling you."

I glanced over at Marlo. She was shaking her head. I did, too.

"Well, the reason Gary's feeling the way he is, is that Dad made him leave school in his senior year when he didn't have to. See, a friend of the family told him he could stay and finish out the year, then come to Florida. But Dad insisted that was too much of an imposition on anyone and said no."

"Oh, wow!" Marlo sighed. "I'd be mad, too. Just think, your senior year."

I frowned. "But you said Gary was planning to do something you didn't think was right. What's that?"

Samantha closed her eyes for a moment as if what she was about to tell us was painful. "I think Dad got to feeling really terrible about the whole situation. So, when he found out that he was going to have to fly to California— that's where we lived—sometime around Easter vacation, he told Gary he could go along, too, and spend the week with his old friends."

"And so?" Marlo asked.

"And so," Samantha went on, "Gary plans to tell my father, just the minute their plane lands in California, that he's staying and that nothing my father does will get him back to Florida."

"How gutsy!" Marlo said, impressed.

"Is Gary old enough to do that?" I asked.

"He'll be eighteen in July. But that's not really the point. See, I just know that this kind of thing would really upset my father. I love my brother, and I'm usually behind him. But I know my father, too. If he does this, my father will really be mad."

Marlo raised her eyebrows. "I see your point."

I could, too. But I didn't say anything. I just looked down at the waves washing up over my toes as I walked along.

"I only wish I could stop him," Samantha said. "But right now I think there's only one person who could."

"Who?" Marlo asked. "Your father?"

"Huh-uh," Samantha shook her head. "Gary's girlfriend." She sighed. "But I don't think she's about to."

"Oh, yeah!" Marlo nodded her head with a kind of sudden understanding. "You're talking about those two letters that got here before you did. The ones on the pink stationery that smelled of Charlie cologne." Marlo pinched her nose together with two fingers. "She must've sprayed the entire bottle on them."

"Yes." Samantha wrinkled her nose. "That's Cynthia all right. She overdoes everything. Including her hold on Gary. She's really got her hooks into him. And I don't think he even realizes it. She's so self-centered, I don't understand what a guy as smart as my brother sees in her. Just because she's pretty!" Samantha made a face. "But I really thought he was wising up just about the time we found out we were to move here. I thought they were about to break up." She shook her head. "I guess Cynthia just couldn't handle the thought of losing him, even to the State of Florida. So she must've put on a brand-new campaign to get him back—and he fell for it. So now, just because of her, he's going to do something really stupid." She shook her head. "He'll be back there in a few months, anyway."

"What do you mean?" Marlo asked curiously.

"Well," Samantha answered, "Gary's planning to go to college in California. He wouldn't even need to wait till September. He could leave right after he graduates from high school here and maybe go to summer school." She shrugged and said, mainly to herself, "So stupid!"

"Gee," Marlo said. "And I was just about to make the supreme sacrifice and let him fall in love with me. He is such a hunk!"

"That's really big of you, Marlo." I crossed my eyes at her. "But somehow I get the impression you aren't really Gary's type."

"No," Samantha agreed. I'd been kidding, but she sounded serious. "Wendy's more Gary's type."

"And just what do you mean by that?" Marlo tried to sound indignant.

"Well, it's true," Samantha said. "You're the outgoing type. Gary's more, well, he's more a one-on-one person. He has a sense of humor, but he doesn't spread it around the way you do. I don't know, I guess what I'm trying to say is that he's fun, but he's also very quiet and sensitive. He's got all these layers of personality that you sometimes have to get through in order to find the real Gary." She looked at me. "I get the feeling that's the way you are, too."

All of a sudden I felt funny about the way the conversation was heading. "Hey," I said to get their attention, "look!" And I pointed. "We're practically there. There's The Hut."

We left the edge of the surf and started across the sand to a group of tables. Kids were lounging around all over, at the tables, on the sand. Halfway there I began feeling shy about the way I'd been acting all week, and I hung back. Marlo saw me, though, and grabbed my arm. "Come on, Wendy. The only way to get back in the swim is to plunge right in."

Roger Mathews, a junior, who is kind of cute but also a bit of a jerk, saw us first and came loping toward our group. When he reached us, he slung a tanned arm across Marlo's shoulders and looked directly at Samantha, leering just a little. "Hey, Marlo," he said in a voice loud enough to be heard two

31

blocks away. "Just who is this gorgeous new body?"

I was about to tell him to cut the stupid come-on, but Samantha beat me to it.

"Hi!" She said in a friendly voice. "I'm Samantha Vries. And for your information, my personality is located in my head, not my body."

At that Roger clutched wildly at his chest. "Aaagh! She got me!" Then he staggered dramatically around before finally falling down, his arms flung out, eyes closed. "I'm dead," he announced, then made a final quiver.

Everyone nearby laughed, including Samantha. She prodded him with a toe. And when he opened one eye, she put out her hand and helped him up. Then, before I could mentally count to ten, the two of them were walking toward the snack shack together so he could buy her a Coke.

Marlo turned to me. "You want to get a Coke?"

"You go ahead," I said. "I'll be right there."

She gave me a friend-to-friend look. "OK, Wendy. But not too long. Or else I'm going to come get you. The idea of bringing you here is to get you back into things, you know."

"I know. I promise, I'll be right there, OK?"

"OK. Just remember, not too long."

There was a low, cement seawall that stretched out from the sand into the surf. I walked over to the other side of it, away from my friends, and sat down, leaning my back against the cool surface. Closing my eyes, I felt the sun dance across my eyelids.

I had to admit I wasn't all that ready to be part of the crowd again yet, despite Marlo's urging. I was still depressed about my mom's leaving, and I didn't much feel like being with people and trying to act cheerful when I wasn't feeling that way.

Suddenly an image of Gary Vries's face swept over me. I thought about how he'd scowled—how I had, too. It was as if he'd put up a mental No Trespassing sign, and in defense I'd put up one, too. But then I remembered how the scowl lines hadn't seemed to fit his face. There were those little white lines that spread out from his eyes in his California tan. They said to me that usually he laughed more than he scowled. And his eyes were nice, the kind of eyes I'd like to get to know better.

I shook my head. *Wendy, I told myself, you're being really silly! The only reason you're thinking about a guy you don't even know is because his sister said he had family problems, too. And if you do keep on thinking about Gary Vries, you're being more than silly. You're being self-destructive. His problems don't have so much to do with his family as with that girl. The one who Samantha said "has her hooks in him." There's no room in Gary's life for anyone*

33

*else, and you'll only get hurt if you think
there is.*

But I couldn't help wondering if Samantha's version of the story of Gary's girlfriend was the way things really were.

Chapter Five

I was walking out of history class scowling at the test I was holding, wondering how I'd managed to get a C when I'd really studied. I almost bumped into Marlo because I wasn't looking where I was going.

"Hey, Wendy," she said peering into my face, "don't frown like that. You'll get wrinkles before you're twenty."

"I've got a right," I retorted. "Just look at this." I shoved the paper toward her. "Do you believe this grade?"

"Oh, don't sweat it! Mr. Wainwright's doing that to everyone these days. I personally think he's going through some kind of midlife crisis." She grabbed the test out of my hand. "Look, forget it."

Suddenly she broke into a wide grin. "I've got something to tell you that will make you forget all about that stupid test."

"OK," I said, grabbing the test paper back and stuffing it into my notebook. "I'll bite. Tell me."

"I'm having a party," she announced, doing a little dance step as we started up the stairs to our lockers.

"A party? What kind of party?"

"For Samantha and Gary, of course." She frowned. "They've been here a week. Don't you think it's about time they had a Welcome-to-Florida party?"

"Oh—well, yeah." I nodded. "I guess so."

"Hey, Wendy," Marlo said as she stopped and gave me a long look, "just how much longer do you plan on being a total drag?"

"What do you mean?" I stopped, too. We were blocking the stairs, and kids weren't too happy about having to walk around us.

"You know what I mean." Marlo glared at one of the kids who had just bumped into us. "When are you going to stop wallowing in self-pity?"

"Huh!" I said. "I suppose you're such an expert on self-pity. What do you know about having problems?"

"Oh, forget it!" She gave me a disgusted look. "Forget I even mentioned the party. I thought you'd like the idea, that's all." She started up the stairs again.

I watched her go. She was right. I had to stop this. "Marlo, Marlo—wait."

She turned around. "I'm sorry," I said, catching up to her. "The party really does sound like fun." I smiled and reached out to link my arm with hers. "Now tell me all about it."

"Oh, OK," she said, pretending still to be mad at me. Then she broke into a smile. "Listen, I'm sorry about what I said, too. It's just that you worry me. You're my closest friend, and I want you to be happy. Besides, it's no fun being around someone who's unhappy all the time." She brightened. "Now—about the party. Oh I'm so excited!" She squeezed my arm as we walked down the hall. "It'll be this Saturday—at night, of course. And I'm going to have it on the patio because I've checked, and there's going to be a full moon. So romantic."

"Sounds great," I said, trying to be enthusiastic.

"You'd better believe it! And listen, you haven't heard the best part." She paused to give a full dramatic effect. "My father's letting me have the Microchips."

"The Microchips?"

"Right." Marlo's voice turned excited. "Remember the band that used to be called the Beach Jocks?"

I nodded.

"Well, they decided they needed a new image, so now they're the Microchips."

"Wow!" I said. "That really is great." I meant it. The party did sound like fun.

"Yep." Marlo grinned. "And remember I said it was going to be romantic. So that means no jeans. If there's going to be a romantic moon, then everyone has to dress accordingly. Hear?"

"I hear," I said.

Standing in the center of the bedroom, staring at my reflection in the mirror, I decided that for the first time since I'd come to live with Aunt Eva, I actually looked as if I belonged in this room.

Obeying Marlo's orders to dress up for her party, I'd put on a dress Aunt Eva had given me for my last birthday. It was the first time I'd worn it because it was too dressy for most of the parties I went to.

It was made of white eyelet, with a full skirt over a pale blue petticoat and pale blue ribbons holding up the camisole top. Stepping over to the mirror, I practiced smiling. I tried to flirt, then I made a face at myself and gave up.

"OK, Wendy," I said aloud to myself, "just who do you think you're kidding? Who are you trying to be romantic for, anyway?"

Just then Aunt Eva knocked on the door and came in. "Oh, Wendy," she said, "you look positively beautiful. Now I really am glad I got that dress for you."

I turned away from the mirror, and feeling suddenly awkward, I smiled at her. "I'm glad you got it for me, too. Do you really think I look OK?"

"OK?" Aunt Eva's eyebrows shot up slightly. "You are going to stun every boy at that party."

"You think so?" I smiled.

"Absolutely." Aunt Eva smiled back. "Now, the reason I came in was to find out if you're almost ready—I can run you over to Marlo's in the car." She winked. "Because I'm going out tonight, too."

"You are?"

"That's right. I'm having dinner with my boss."

"Oh." I sort of shrugged. "Your boss."

"But remember." She grinned. "I knew him before he became my boss." Then she kind of danced toward the door. "I'll go get the car," she said over her shoulder.

I was happy for her. I had to remember to be sure and tell her how nice she looked when I got out of the car at Marlo's. I turned back to the dresser and reached to pick up the white clutch purse Aunt Eva had lent me for the evening. As I did, my hand happened to brush against the still unopened letter of Mom's that I'd left lying on the back of the dresser. I looked down at the letter. Why did I have to notice it? It was almost as if Mom were purposely trying to spoil the party for me. Well, I wouldn't let her. Quickly I grabbed the letter, opened the top drawer, shoved the letter way in the back, and slammed the drawer shut.

Taking a deep breath, I picked up the

clutch purse, then ran through the house and out the front door. In no time I slid into the front seat beside Aunt Eva and shut the door safely behind me.

The party was already under way by the time Aunt Eva dropped me off. Marlo had strung tiny, colored Christmas-tree lights all through the lemon and orange trees that lined each side of the flagstone pavement. And Japanese lanterns were strung in a crisscross pattern over the area cleared for dancing. The Microchips had set up near the low wall that separated the patio from the beach, and they were playing a fast song.

I paused near the edge of the dance area and watched several couples. Suddenly two hands grabbed me around the waist from behind, and a voice said, "Gotcha" in my ear.

I let out a little scream and twisted around to find myself staring into the freckled face of Charlie Evans. "Oh, hi!" I said, trying not to groan.

Charlie Evans was not someone you would pick to start an evening at a party with. He was nice, and his looks, despite the freckles, were OK. It was just that his personality would have benefited from a major overhaul. There were times when he acted as if he were still in the sixth grade.

"Cool party, huh?" Charlie grinned, continuing to hold on to me.

"Right!" I nodded.

He grinned some more. I looked down at his hands, then back up to his face. "Charlie, you can let go of me now. I promise I won't run away."

"Oh, yeah, ha-ha," Charlie answered. But I had to pry his fingers away before he really understood that I meant what I said.

"That's a pretty dress."

"Thank you," I said politely. Behind Charlie's shoulder I could see Marlo dancing with Andy Witherspoon. And beyond them, sitting beneath a banner reading "Welcome to Florida, Samantha and Gary," were Samantha and Roger. They were looking at each other in a way that made me pretty sure neither one of them was about to leap up and rescue me from Charlie.

Then I made the mistake of making accidental eye contact with Stephanie Henderson. How did she manage to crash the party? I knew Marlo would certainly never have invited her. But, then, if Stephanie wanted to go somewhere, she always managed to get an invitation. She smiled at me, a kind of saccharine smile, all bitter aftertaste. But what was worse was that she started to walk directly toward me. I thought fast.

"Let's dance!" I grabbed Charlie's arm.

"Huh?" Charlie said. But he didn't have time to say anything else. I towed him onto the dance floor.

The group was playing another fast number, and before we started to dance, I took one last look at Stephanie. She stopped and was standing there looking at me with crossed arms and narrowed eyes. Ignoring her, I flashed a smile at Charlie. It was then that I remembered Charlie couldn't dance. He was positively dangerous.

"This group is too much, right?" he said, stepping on someone's foot. "Ooops—sorry!"

"Right! They're really great." I nodded, dodging an outflung arm.

"Ooops—sorry," Charlie said again. This time it was my foot he'd stepped on.

"No problem." I moved away from him only to step on someone else's foot myself. I closed my eyes long enough to send a silent prayer to the band to hurry up and finish the number. And someone up there was listening. Roger tapped Charlie on the shoulder.

"Hey, old buddy," he said to Charlie, "mind if I cut in?"

Charlie frowned and looked at Roger, then at me. "Is that OK with you, Wendy?"

"Yes, I guess," I said, trying to look as if I were really sorry to lose him as a dance partner. "We can dance again later." I smiled at him as he backed off the floor.

"Thanks," I told Roger, falling into step with him.

"It's really Samantha you should thank," he said, nodding to where she was sitting, still under the banner. "She said you looked like you were about to go down for the third time."

"I think I was," I said, laughing. I smiled over at Samantha, gave her a little wave, and mouthed "thanks." She grinned back and mouthed "anytime."

The dance ended, and the group started a slow number. Roger remarked, "I think we'd better forget this one. Saving you from Charlie was one thing, but I don't think Samantha would appreciate my dancing a slow number with you. I think I should save those for her."

"Right," I agreed.

"Thanks for sending your knight in shining armor," I told Samantha as Roger and I crossed over to her.

"Well," she said and smiled, "you did look pretty desperate." She turned to Roger. "OK, knight in shining armor, would you be so kind as to get your fair maiden a Coke or something? I'm positively dying of thirst."

As soon as Roger left, Samantha became anxious. "Wendy, have you seen Gary anywhere?"

"Gary?" I shook my head. "But I haven't really been here that long. Why, what's the matter?"

Samantha frowned. "I think he's missing. I haven't seen him since the party started. I don't know whether to be furious because he's being rude and staying away, or worried that something might have happened to him. You know how he's been since we got here."

"Are you positive he isn't just someplace you haven't looked?" I asked. "You know how it can be at a party with everyone milling around."

"Well—" She looked doubtful. "Maybe—"

"Here comes Roger," I said, looking up. "Why don't you tell him, let him look around."

"Huh-uh," Samantha whispered. "I don't want to alarm anyone just yet. But if you do see Gary, tell him I'm looking for him, will you?"

"Sure," I said just as Roger came up. Samantha gave Roger a big smile and took the drink he'd brought.

"Hey," I said, smiling for Roger's benefit as well, "I think I'll go check out the food. Marlo's parents usually put out a great spread." I gave a little wave. "And I'll be sure to give Gary your message."

As I walked away, I heard Roger asking what my last remark had been about and Samantha's phony-sounding answer that it wasn't anything really.

Now I was wondering, too.

I hadn't really intended to go to the buffet table; that had been an excuse to get away. Instead I walked over the low wall that separated the patio from the beach and sat down. There was a large, romantic moon illuminating a path on the Gulf. I frowned at it.

Where *was* Gary?

I had to admit to myself that I hadn't spent all that time getting ready for the party just to turn on someone like Charlie Evans. I'd wanted to impress Gary Vries. Sure, there was that girl in California, but things had happened in the last week, and maybe that had changed. Marlo had said there hadn't been any more letters since the first two. And Gary had actually smiled at me twice. OK, both times were at school when we were both in a crowd. But a smile is a smile. It beats a scowl anytime. But how was I supposed to stun him if he wasn't around to see me?

The Microchips were taking a break, and behind me people were standing around talking. I overheard a couple of girls, and after a minute I realized they were talking about Gary. "He's such a hunk, isn't he?"

"Oh, yeah," came the answer. "On a scale of one to ten, he is definitely a nine."

"Gary Vries?" another girl's voice suddenly broke in. "Huh-uh, he's no nine, he's definitely a full ten."

"OK," the first voice admitted, "you're right. But where is he, anyway? I haven't seen him since we got here."

"Maybe," someone suggested, "he's already found a matching ten, and they've gone someplace where it's more romantic, if you know what I mean!" At that the other two giggled. I shut them out, not wanting to hear any more.

The Microchips had come back and were playing a new piece, a love song. The lights in the lemon trees winked on and off, making little dime-sized dots of color on the sand. I felt as if I had to get away. I slipped off my shoes and started down the beach in my stocking feet.

As I left the lights of the party behind, the moonlight turned the landscape to silver and black. The sea oats on the dunes became gently waving blades of silver, while black waves, tipped with silver foam, curled onto the sand.

I'd walked a long way without running into another person. Ahead of me was a small wooden pier. I could see the outline of two pelicans perched on a piece of broken railing. I walked quietly around the end of the pier so I wouldn't disturb them. I almost didn't see the other person standing there in the shadows. But when he stepped out farther onto the beach, I could see who it was. Gary. I stopped still so he wouldn't see me.

He was facing the Gulf, hands thrust into his pockets, the bottom of his pants rolled up as if he'd been walking along the edge of the water.

Something startled the pelicans, and they suddenly soared off into the night sky, two silhouettes briefly crossing the moon before they disappeared.

Gary turned around and saw me.

"Were you following me?"

"No—no." I shook my head.

"Then what are you doing here? You were watching me."

"No," I said again. A quick breeze blew in from the water, and my skirt billowed out around me. "I just came around the pier, and there you were. I was about to leave, but you happened to see me before I could."

He came closer. "Did Samantha send you looking for me?"

"No." A breeze slid over my bare shoulders, and I shivered.

"You didn't answer my question. What are you doing here?"

"Look!" I found myself getting angry. "This is a public beach. It isn't yours exclusively."

"Oh, really!"

"Right!"

"Well!" He stopped, not saying anything for a few seconds. "Hey," he said, his voice changing so it didn't sound so angry anymore, "you're right. I'm sorry I jumped on you the way I did."

But his apology went sailing right past me. Once I was angry, it was hard for me to calm down. So instead of saying, "That's OK," I yelled at him even more. "Listen," I said, "don't you know just how rude you're being by staying away? Don't you realize how much

47

trouble Marlo went to to arrange the party for you? Honestly!" I'd spread my feet out, and my toes were curling tightly into the sand. "And do you realize that your sister is really worried about you? No, I suppose that wouldn't even occur to you. I bet all you can think about is your own little set of problems. Well, let me tell you, you're not the only one with problems. Everyone has them. I have them. But you wouldn't find me being so self-centered that I'd ruin a party for everyone else by going off to sulk. You know what I think? I think—"

"Hey—whoa!" Gary interrupted. He reached out to touch me. But I jumped back.

"Furthermore," I went on without thinking, "I think you and that girl in California probably deserve each other." Suddenly I realized what I'd said and came to a halt.

"Huh—what?"

"You heard me," I said, only in a much lower voice. I was really wishing my impulsive mouth had wound down before this.

"Who told you about my—the girl in California?"

"Oh, everyone knows," I said, feeling totally stupid now.

"Listen, about that girl—"

But I didn't want to listen. I shook my head, then turned and stalked away.

48

Chapter Six

Sunday morning was my favorite time for jogging on the beach. If I got out early enough, the beach was generally empty—just one or two local joggers. We'd nod to one another and jog on. If the tide was going out, I'd run along the wide band of damp sand left by the retreating surf.

The morning after the party, the sun was just coming up when I started out, and it streaked the sky with orange and pink. A pack of sea gulls circled lazily out over the water.

I was wearing an old sweat shirt, faded shorts, and no shoes. I was barefoot because that's the way I liked to run. It was still cool, so there were tiny goose bumps on my legs.

I'd run about two blocks and was just getting warmed up when I saw a familiar figure jogging toward me. It wasn't until he got closer, though, that I recognized Gary Vries.

"Oh, no!" I moaned to myself as a complete version of what I'd said to him the night before on the beach played through my head. I made a sudden wish that a very deep hole would materialize in front of me so I could step into it and never be heard of again.

But that didn't happen. What did happen was that we got closer and closer to each other. Watching him running barefoot toward me, all tanned muscle moving gracefully, I couldn't believe I'd had the nerve to tell him off the way I had. Why was it that I always seemed to have lots of courage at night, and the next day it all went *pop*?

I wondered if it would look too obvious if I turned around and went the other way. I decided quickly that it would. By then we were close, so close I could make out his features.

Just then I thought about all those commercials where the boy and girl run slowly into each other's arms. Wouldn't it be funny if we did that?

As we were about to pass each other, Gary gave me a sudden smile. I was so surprised I wasn't sure what to do.

Smile back, you idiot! I screamed silently to myself. I smiled.

"Morning," he huffed as he passed.

My heart stopped for a whole second. I caught my breath and said back, "Hi, nice morning, huh?" But Gary was gone.

I couldn't believe it! I couldn't believe what had just happened.

But right away I started thinking, *Wendy, you jerk—why didn't you come up with something more original to say?* And then I started worrying about whether my face had been red or the muscles in my legs had wobbled or my hair had been a mess. And why hadn't I put lip gloss on before I'd left the house? And why hadn't I worn the new pink sweat shirt Aunt Eva had bought me?

Just then I heard the thud of feet coming up behind me. I decided it was another jogger, and I moved over so he or she could pass me. But I was wrong. It was him!

"Hey." He looked over at me. "What did you say back there?"

"Huh?"

"Back there." He motioned his thumb. "You said something else. And I couldn't figure out what it was."

I shook my head, also breathing hard. "I just said it was a nice morning."

"Oh!" He nodded again. "Yeah, it is!"

"What?"

"A good morning!"

"Oh, yeah!" I nodded.

I kept running. I sort of expected him to turn back.

"About last night—"

Oh, darn! Here it was, time for him to tell me what he thought of what I'd said. *Hole,* I prayed, *where are you?*

He started again. "About last night, what I want to know is, do you always come on that strong?" I glanced over toward him, noticing

51

the smile lines were there, around his eyes. There wasn't any scowl. He glanced back, and I saw the lines deepen. "Or is it only in special cases—like mine?"

"Uh—*special cases*," I finally managed to choke out. I smiled, wondering what he would do back.

He grinned. "I kind of thought that might be the case." We ran a few more steps. "Anyway, I'm glad we met this morning. I wanted to tell you last night that I agree with you. I *was* acting like a self-centered jerk." He huffed, getting his breath. "But you tore off."

I tried hard to think of something to say back, but I couldn't. So, instead, I huffed a lot, pretending to be too much out of breath to answer him.

"And when I tried to find you later, at the party, you'd left. How come?"

What I did then was really brilliant. I blushed. I blushed all the way through my tan. And he noticed.

"Hey, are you mad again?"

"N-no," I stuttered and shook my head to show I wasn't.

The only problem with shaking your head as violently as I was doing is that, when you're jogging, especially on the beach, there are certain hazards—like the clump of seaweed I tripped on and fell over.

Next thing I knew, he was standing over

me, holding out both hands and helping me up.

We continued to hold hands.

"*Pax?*" he said in his low, smooth voice. He was barely huffing.

"*Pax!*" I nodded.

He dropped my hands then and put his on his hips. "Well, I'm glad that's taken care of. Now, how about finishing our run? It's bad to stop without cooling down, you know."

"I know," I agreed. We started down the beach again. He'd said *our* run. Gary had said *our*!

Oh, wow!

He wasn't self-centered after all.

I felt warm all over. Mostly, though, in the center of my stomach, so I knew it wasn't just because I was running. I looked ahead of me, pretending to concentrate on my form.

We ran another mile, then both of us began to slow down to a walk. The beach wasn't empty any longer. Some tourists were beginning to come out and put down their towels. And a lot of people were just wandering up and down the damp sand, looking for shells. Normally I do that, check for new shells to add to my collection as I walk back from jogging. But that morning, shells were about the farthest thing from my mind. I was walking along the beach with Gary.

Gary bent down and picked up a shell. He held it out for me to see. It was a star shell, a nice one, whorled, with sawlike spines and a beautiful, silvery-white color.

"That's a long-spined star," I explained.

"Hmmm, yes." He nodded absently. "I know."

"Hey!" I looked at him and grinned. " Do you like shells, too?"

"Uh-huh, sure do." He polished the shell on the sleeve of his sweat shirt, then slipped it into the pocket of his shorts. "You do, too, huh? But I guess that'd be only natural considering you live practically right on the beach."

"Maybe," I said. "But I'm the only one in my group who does. Oh, when we were little, everyone collected them. But after a while I guess everyone else got bored with them."

"But you didn't?"

"No." I rolled my eyes. "You should see my room. I'm really into them. I've got them all—" All at once I stopped in midsentence, remembering the room I was describing didn't exist anymore. My entire collection was carefully packed away in boxes and stored in Aunt Eva's hall closet.

"Where do you have them, on shelves?" Gary was asking.

"I did—I mean, I do," I blurted out, deciding I didn't want to have to go into a lengthy explanation.

"That's the way I used to keep mine. But then I found this set of instructions in a magazine on how to build glass display cases," he said enthusiastically. "And now you should see how they look—really great." He paused, his brow furrowing. "Or, they did. I forgot. Everything is all packed away in storage along with the rest of the family furniture and stuff."

"Your shells, too?"

"Well, no." He shook his head. "Not my shells. I brought them with me on the plane. I wasn't about to trust them to the moving company."

"Boy, do I understand," I said. "I have shells I wouldn't let a stranger carry across the room."

"Yeah," he agreed. "I know what you mean."

We were quiet for a bit. But this time the quiet was the comfortable kind. Then Gary pulled out his shell again. "I'm glad I found this. It's my first official find in the Carolinian-Caribbean Province." He rubbed the shell affectionately before putting it back. "See," he explained, "most of my collection is from the Californian Province. Though I do have a couple from the Indo-Pacific. But that's only because we spent some time in Hawaii last summer."

"Oh, wow!" I was awed. Not because Gary had been to Hawaii, but because he knew that shell areas were divided into zones called provinces. If I mentioned the word *province* to any of my friends, they'd think I was talking in a foreign language.

"Well, yeah, Hawaii's a great place," Gary said, obviously misunderstanding. "You'd like it there. It's like Florida in a way, but with a lot more trees, or something." He shrugged. "It's hard to explain."

"Well, my collection's strictly from around here." I smiled at him.

"Hey, would you like to see my collection sometime?" He sounded pleased. I had a feeling he had friends like mine who didn't understand.

"Sure," I said. "I mean it."

"Great!"

I held my breath, waiting for him to name a time and place. But he didn't. Instead, he bent down and picked up another shell. "Do you like top shells?" he asked.

"Um-hmm," I answered. "But I don't have that many."

He turned and casually skimmed the shell he'd been holding out over the water. "I have a queen tegula." The way he said it, he wasn't bragging. He didn't have to. The result was the same as if he'd spelled the word out in neon letters.

"A queen tegula!"

"Yeah," he said, grinning. "I found it myself, too. I didn't buy it in any store. See, I don't believe in buying shells. My feeling is

56

that anyone can do that. Finding them your-self is what's really important."

"That's exactly how I feel!" I said excitedly. "That's why my collection is only from this province."

We'd reached Marlo's patio wall and stopped automatically. Gary kicked at the sand while I hugged my arms around my waist, trying to think up some great exit line.

"Hey, listen, Gary." I hugged myself even tighter. "You know, if you really want a great place to look for shells, there's this island, Sand Crab Key, not too far from here. It's con-sidered one of the best places in the entire world for shelling. Maybe you'd like to go there with me sometime."

The minute I said it, I wanted to bury myself in the sand. I'd just intended to sound friendly, but it must've sounded like I was hinting for a date.

"Oh." He frowned slightly, looking into my eyes. "Do you go there very often?"

"Huh-uh," I shook my head. "I don't have a car. You really need one to get there. There isn't any bus that runs early in the morning, and you have to get there practically before the sun comes up. If you wait any longer, all the good shells are gone. Lots of people go there. Lots!" *Wendy*, I told myself, *your mouth is racing. Shut up.*

"Well, I don't have a car," Gary said. "Not here." My stomach went cold. He was politely

57

telling me there was no way he wanted to go anywhere with me.

"Oh," I said, my voice so low I could barely hear it myself.

"But my dad's got a rental car," Gary went on. "And he hardly ever uses it on Saturday. So how about then? Next Saturday. You want to go?"

"Saturday?" I put my hand up to my forehead as if I were trying to think what was happening next Saturday. "Well, uh, sure." I smiled. "I'd love to go."

"Great!" He grinned. "Then it's a date. Next Saturday."

"Yeah, Saturday," I agreed.

I was still trying to find an exit line. I crossed my arms again and stared down at my toes. Oh, my gosh! Half of them had pink polish on them, half didn't. I'd really meant to do something about that. I looked back up. Gary wasn't paying any attention to my toes.

"Saturday?"

"Saturday!" I pulled my arms apart and danced backward a couple of steps. "Well—see you in school then." I turned around and started walking, very conscious of the way I was moving.

"Hey, Wendy!" he called after me. "By the way, I liked the dress you were wearing last night."

My face practically split open in a grin, and I felt as if someone had just handed me a marvelous Christmas present. But I forced the grin into a casual smile and turned around just long enough to say, "Thank you," then sort of tossed my head in the sophisticated way Marlo does before turning back away.

"Saturday, Saturday, Saturday," I hummed to myself all the way home, almost like the word was some kind of special lyric to a very special song.

Chapter Seven

When the alarm went off the next morning, I woke up feeling wonderful and slightly fuzzy. I wasn't quite awake yet, but I knew something good had happened. I reached over, shut off the alarm, and lay still staring up at the ceiling. I tried to remember what was making me so happy. Then I knew: Gary had asked me for a date.

Maybe it wasn't an honest-to-goodness date—and I really had been the one who'd done the asking. But hadn't he said the word *date*, and wasn't that what counted? Sure. This was the eighties. You weren't supposed to hang around, waiting breathlessly for some guy to get up the nerve to ask you out.

I sat up and hugged my knees. The real thing, though, was how Gary felt. *Face it, Wendy*, I told myself, *there's still that girl in California.* But she was three thousand miles away! Still, what's three thousand miles when you're in love? But maybe he wasn't really in love. Who said he was in love, anyway? Gary?

Actually it had been Samantha. And all she'd had to go on were those two pink letters that arrived for Gary before he even got here. Pink letters. Pink letters smelling of Charlie! I flopped back down on the bed, my arms flung out to the sides. Pink letters! Just who did I think I was kidding?

Still, I was very picky about deciding what to wear to school. Standing in front of the open closet, I mentally tried on just about everything I owned. I finally settled on a white, almost-silk blouse, my red cords, and white sandals.

I skipped breakfast because the cords felt a bit on the tight side. Walking past Aunt Eva, who was sitting at the table, hands wrapped around a cup of coffee, I sucked in my breath, hoping she wouldn't make the suggestion that I go back and put something else on. But all she did was smile and say, "You look especially nice today, Wendy." Then, "Have a good day."

Walking to the corner where I normally met Marlo—and now Samantha as well—I suddenly developed a pinched feeling in the pit of my stomach. So much had happened between Gary and me since Saturday night, I'd almost forgotten about having left the party early without an explanation. But how could I explain that I'd gone hiking out on the beach in my stocking feet, then ended up telling off my best friend's house guest, and gotten so upset because of it that I'd walked home without bothering to go back to the party to get my shoes?

I'd also have to tell Marlo about meeting Gary on the beach Sunday morning and that we'd made up and even had a sort-of date. I just wasn't ready to discuss that with anyone, not even my best friend. No, make that *especially* my best friend. Because I was afraid she'd tell me he was still hung up on that girl in California and that my going on even a sort-of date with him would make me a boyfriend snatcher.

But then I told myself I was probably creating a problem where there wasn't one. Probably Marlo had been so busy being a good hostess, as well as dancing with Andy Witherspoon, that she hadn't even noticed I was missing.

However, now that I was closer, I could see Marlo was standing the way she did when she was annoyed, with one hip stuck out and an angry thumb gripped around the strap of her backpack. Also, her mouth definitely had turned-down corners.

"All right, Wendy," she started in on me just as soon as I was within hearing range, "just exactly where did you disappear to Saturday night? And where were you all day yesterday? I practically punched the numbers off the phone trying to get you."

"Hi, Marlo!" I smiled at her casually. "Where's Samantha?"

"Huh?"

"Samantha. Is she sick? How come she isn't here with you?"

"Don't change the subject. What's going on with *you*?"

"Samantha," I reminded her.

"Oh . . ." She waved the hand that wasn't clutching at the strap in a vague way. "Roger drove her to school. He's helping her catch up on chemistry or something." She scowled. "Who cares? I want to know why you ducked out of my party."

"I really thought your party was fabulous. The lights in the trees were positively fantastic. Your mom always makes great food. And the Microchips were a positive triumph. I mean they were *great*! The great—"

"So why didn't you stay?"

"Listen, I'm sorry. I had to go." I thought quickly. "My aunt wasn't feeling well, and she asked if I'd come home early. You know how it is when you've got the flu and you're really feeling rotten? You want someone there to get you a drink of water, or something—"

I broke off as we crossed at a corner, dodging a couple of guys on ten-speeds.

"Yeah, sure."

"Well—" I added lamely. I knew Marlo wasn't buying my story. But then she surprised me by jumping to a totally different conclusion.

"You know, you've really got to stop this moping around. Just because you didn't have a date for the party didn't mean you couldn't enjoy yourself. I saw you dancing with Charlie Evans. I know he's not the greatest, but he is a guy. I mean—"

"Sorry," I said. "Charlie Evans is just about the last person I'd be interested in. Look, right now—"

"OK, OK," Marlo shrugged. "Forget I asked." Then she looked at me with a puzzled expression. "Did you leave your shoes at my house? Gary found some out by the wall. He said he thought they might be yours." She frowned. "What I don't understand is how would he know? I mean, as far as I can remember when you were at the party, he wasn't. And when he showed up again, you'd already gone. If I didn't know better—"

"Shoes?" I broke in before she could get into any heavy speculation. "Someone left her shoes? Oh, how hysterical!" I laughed. Or tried to. I shook my head. "How would I have gotten home without my shoes? And speaking of shoes, that's where I was yesterday. Shopping."

"Shopping?"

"Right. My aunt and I went shopping at the mall. There were some great sales. I got this pair of pink sneakers to go with my new sweat shirt. You know, the one I got—"

"Wait a second!" Marlo stopped still and put one hand on her waist. "What was your aunt doing going shopping when she had the flu?"

"Oh—uh—she had the twenty-four-hour kind. You know, one second you feel all horrible, the next you're dying to go someplace because you're tired of staying in bed. All I know is she wanted to go shopping, and we went." I'm so bad at trying to put lies together.

I saw Marlo beginning to frown. Thankfully we were close to school, and I looked around for the first person I could see to wave to. "Oh, look!" I chattered. "There's Charlie Evans!" I raised my hand and waved. "Hi, Charlie!"

It wasn't until after Charlie had heard me and looked over with a happy look on his face and waved back that I realized exactly whom I'd waved to.

But Marlo had picked up on it right away. "Ah-ha! So you don't really think much of Charlie Evans, huh?" She nodded her head. "Now I see. I see it all. And that's why you're wearing your red cords today. You want to look terrific for Charlie!" She practically sang the last sentence.

"Marlo!" I hissed. "Keep it down, please. Someone might hear you." I felt my face getting hot. "I just thought it was about time to wear something different, that's all."

"Um-hmm," Marlo grunted. But we'd

reached the front steps of school, and Marlo dropped the subject. "Hey," she said, "you want to go to the bathroom to check your hair, or anything?"

"Uh, no." I shook my head. My face had cooled down. "I'd better not. I've an oral report in English first period, and I think I'd better get to class early so I can go over my notes. I'm not exactly all that prepared."

"Oh, wow!" Marlo patted me sympathetically on the shoulder. "Good luck! Oral reports—bleah!" She made a face. "Well, see you at lunch." She started up the steps, then stopped and called back over her shoulder. "And good luck impressing *whoever* it is you want to impress. You do look good."

But I might as well have worn a gunny-sack all day. I walked miles through all the halls, and I didn't run into Gary once. Charlie Evans, drooling slightly, made a comment about my looking sexy. But as far as I was concerned, it was a waste. And to think I had had only iced tea for lunch because my pants were too tight!

Tuesday was just as bad. Actually, it was probably worse. I was wearing my second-best outfit, light blue designer jeans, a light blue tank top with lace edging and my highest-heeled sandals. I was walking down the hall when I saw Gary. We were only about ten feet away from each other. He was going into class.

I don't know how he could have missed

seeing me, but he acted as if I were totally transparent. At first I couldn't believe it. Then I finally convinced myself that he probably had something on his mind.

By Wednesday I'd run out of my really best things to wear. I was back to my blue denim wraparound skirt and a plaid blouse, which, unfortunately, I'd stained when I'd eaten a chocolate bar at morning break.

Samantha and I were walking to computer science class when we rounded a corner and practically bumped into Gary. He was by himself, and he didn't look as if he were in a big hurry.

So I took the opportunity and jumped in with both feet. "Hi, Gary," I said. "Find any good shells lately?" I smiled, practically oozing charm.

For a second he looked startled, as if he weren't expecting to see us. Which I guess was true, considering we'd nearly run him down. But instead of relaxing, he got all stiff and kind of polite.

"Oh, hi, Sam," he said in the general direction of where Samantha was standing. Then he frowned slightly and said in my direction, "Hi—uh—ah—"

"Wendy," I prompted him, my charm definitely cooling.

"Yes, sure," he answered me. "Well." His frown deepened. "I've got to get going, or I'll be late for physics." And he took off.

I glanced over toward Samantha. "Did I say something wrong?"

Her mouth tightened into a straight line. "No, Wendy, no." She shook her head. "He's acting dumb again. And I thought he was getting back to normal. Well, come on, or we'll be late for class ourselves." She took my arm. "Honestly, brothers!" she muttered.

I followed Samantha into class and sat down. Although computer science was one of my favorite classes, I couldn't pay attention. Samantha even had to hit my shoulder to get my attention when the instructor called my name; I was that bad. I kept wondering what was wrong with Gary. Something had to have happened since Sunday. But what?

The only answer that I kept coming up with was the girl in California. Had she called him on the phone? Had she written him more letters?

I was confused and silent for the rest of the day. Samantha asked me what was wrong. She really sounded concerned. But I told her it was nothing, that I just had a headache. I'm not sure she believed me, but what could she say?

I told Marlo the same thing. But she wouldn't let it go. She gave me this look and said, "You never get headaches."

"Well, I've got one now," I said coldly.

"Well, OK!" She raised one eyebrow. "You

don't have to snap at me." Then she let the matter drop.

I felt guilty about the way I was acting, but I couldn't help it. The way the day was steadily sliding downhill, I wondered what could possibly happen next.

I found out when I got home from school. First there was a note on the refrigerator door telling me that Mom had called. And there was a number where I could call her back. Well, I told myself, getting an apple out of the crisper and shutting the door hard enough to make the note fall off the door, I wasn't going to do that. As far as I was concerned, Mom had wasted her money calling in the first place. I wasn't going to waste Aunt Eva's money calling her back. Then I went into the bedroom and found a new letter from Mom sitting on my dresser.

I sighed, put the half-eaten apple down, and picked up the envelope. It was a lot fatter than the first letter. I turned it over. On the back flap she'd scrawled S.W.A.K. A flood of guilt swept over me, and I opened my dresser drawer and jammed the letter in with the first one. Then I slammed the drawer shut.

What was I feeling so guilty about, anyway? After all, Mom had left me, hadn't she? It wasn't the other way around. I picked up the apple again. But I wasn't hungry anymore. I threw it in the trash.

The next morning I was in the middle of

putting on a sock, trying hard not to think about Mom, when the reason for Gary's big freeze came to me. It was so obvious. Why hadn't I figured it out before?

It was simple. I'd been aggressive. I'd been the one to suggest going shell hunting, practically insisting that we make it a date. Gary probably didn't like aggressive girls. But he'd been too polite to turn me down. Then all week long he'd tried to show me he didn't want to go by acting cool toward me. I'd been too stupid to get the message. And he probably pretended to forget my name just so I'd finally get the point. Wendy—Wendy! I hit myself on the forehead with my sock. *What a jerk you are! You have completely ruined any possible future chance you might have had with him!*

After that I was in such a funk I ended up putting on the first thing I could find—a blouse with a rip on one shoulder and a button missing, and a pair of jeans so old I wouldn't ordinarily wear them to dig clams.

When I met Marlo on the corner, she laughed. "Good grief, who are you trying to impress this morning?"

"No one," I said sulkily.

"Humph! Well, you've definitely succeeded."

I just glared at her.

"Oh, come off it, Wendy," Marlo said, sighing. "Please don't start being a pain again. What's the matter, anyway? Did you hear from your mother or something?"

70

I glared at her one more time.

"Oh, brother!" She rolled her eyes. "Here we go again!"

We walked the rest of the way to school in absolute silence. Halfway up the front steps Marlo stopped and turned to say, "Look, Wendy, just snap out of it. OK? Just snap out of it! And for goodness' sake, stop dressing like that. You look terrible."

"Oh, thanks, Marlo—thanks a million," I said, my eyes narrowing. "You're sure one to talk. You always dress like you just stepped off the cover of a fashion magazine, right? Ha!"

She put her hands on her hips. "Well, at least I don't come to school looking like a walking advertisement for Goodwill Industries."

"Ha! Listen, Marlo Williams, if you're so ashamed to be seen with me, then just stay away."

"Hey, I think I'll just do that!" Marlo snapped. "At least until you've decided to come to your senses and be yourself again." She ran to the top of the steps. "Please, Wendy, just get real. I don't want to have to find another best friend, but I will!" Then she was gone.

Watching her go, I scowled. What was going on? Everyone was avoiding me. It was like I had the plague or something.

Just then a sticky sweet voice crooned in my ear. "Hello, Wendy, dear."

I whirled around, and there stood Stephanie Henderson, an expression of total satisfaction on her face. She'd overheard everything. I had a feeling she couldn't wait to spread the news. I scowled at her.

She looked at me, all innocence. "Is there a problem? Is there anything I can do to help?"

I thought I was going to strangle her. I could feel the blood begin to tingle through my veins, faster and faster. I'd heard of people reaching a breaking point. Was this what it felt like?

There were other kids standing on the steps. And some of them were watching us. But it didn't matter. I was past caring if I made a scene or not. I stared straight at Stephanie.

"Yes," I said, my voice surprisingly calm considering what was going on inside me, "you can stop playing reporter for the *National Enquirer* because my personal life is absolutely none of your business. That's what you can do to help. I only hope you're capable of understanding what I'm saying. But, frankly, I wouldn't bet on it!"

Stephanie's mouth popped open. I didn't wait for an answer. I turned around and stomped up the stairs.

As I went through the front door, I think I heard a smattering of applause. But I was so surprised at myself for having the nerve to tell off Stephanie Henderson, I didn't care. I felt great.

Chapter Eight

Marlo and I mutually avoided each other for the rest of the day. By the time I'd walked home all alone, I was positively miserable. It had been a kind of triumph to finally tell Stephanie what I thought of her. But it would have been a lot better if I'd been able to tell Marlo about it.

I was quiet all through dinner, and Aunt Eva must have known there was something wrong, but she didn't pry. Afterward I didn't go into the living room to watch TV with her; I went to my room instead.

The phone rang about seven. I heard Aunt Eva answer it, then come down the hall. She knocked on the door. "It's Marlo. She says it's important that she talk to you."

"I don't want to talk to her," I said. "Tell her I'm dead or something."

Aunt Eva waited for a couple of seconds before she gave up and walked back to the phone.

A few minutes later she was back, and

this time she came into my room and walked over to my bed. I was lying on my stomach staring at the carpet, my head hanging over the edge of the bed. She sat down beside me and put her hand on my back.

"Did you and Marlo have a falling out?"

I nodded. "Sort of." I was still looking at the carpet.

"Umm." She rubbed my back. "What's worse? What you said to each other or why you said it? Of course, you don't have to tell me if it isn't any of my business. But I'd be happy to listen, if you think it would help."

"Oh, I don't know," I said, then rolled over and stared at the ceiling. "Everything's mixed up. I guess I'm not ready to talk about it yet."

"OK." Aunt Eva nodded. "But, remember, I'm always here in case you ever want to talk."

"I'm kind of afraid Marlo doesn't want to be my best friend anymore," I said miserably.

"Oh?" Aunt Eva said gently.

I frowned. "And I'm not sure how I feel, either." I rolled over onto my side and rested my head on one hand. "The thing is, she's acting weird. I used to be able to count on her when I had a problem. And now I just get the feeling she couldn't care less."

"Do you think maybe she doesn't really understand?" Aunt Eva asked. "Maybe you just didn't take the time to really explain."

"No!" I shook my head and sat up. I'd suddenly realized I hadn't explained anything at all. I was the one who wasn't being fair. I'd never let her know how badly I was hurt by my mom leaving, and I hadn't confided in her about Gary, either. I'd been expecting Marlo to understand things that she knew nothing about. And it was because, for the first time in our friendship, I hadn't wanted to confide in her. "Aunt Eva, I didn't tell her anything," I confessed. "I don't know, I couldn't. Oh—" I ended miserably.

"Wendy." Aunt Eva smiled encouragingly. "You know, being best friends doesn't mean you have to share everything. It just means you share most things. And sometimes keeping problems to yourself can be a very adult thing to do. It means you're not counting on someone else to do your thinking and problem-solving for you."

"Oh?" I said, trying to absorb Aunt Eva's advice. It sounded very logical. "But what about Marlo? Maybe she's upset because she thinks I've been standoffish."

"Well," Aunt Eva said, patting my shoulder, "I wouldn't worry too much about that. From the way she sounded on the phone, I got the distinct impression she was feeling bad about what happened today and wanted to talk to you about it." She stood up. "But I told her you'd gone to bed early and no doubt you'd meet her in the usual place in the morning."

"Then you didn't tell her I was dead?"

"Come on, Wendy, really!" Aunt Eva

laughed. "Do you think she would believe something like that?"

"No." I laughed back. "I'm glad you told her what you did. Thank you."

"Sure!" Aunt Eva smiled and walked to the door. "By the way, your mother called again today. She said you never called her back yesterday. I told her it was because you probably couldn't get through. Did you try?"

"Uh, uh, yeah, sure." I nodded, protesting so much that Aunt Eva had to see I was lying. "I tried, but the number was busy."

"Ummm." She frowned, nodding. "Well, she'll probably call back tomorrow." Then she smiled. "You get some sleep now. I'm sure everything will look a lot better in the morning. It always does." She blew me a kiss before closing the door behind her.

I sat staring at the door, thinking about the last thing she'd said. I wasn't at all sure things were going to look so great in the morning. And I should have told her right out that I didn't want to talk to Mom at all. If she wanted to, she could tell Mom that.

Instead, I'd lied. I sighed. Then I stood up and started getting ready for bed.

The dream was horrible. It was still vivid when I opened my eyes and stared into the gray, dim bedroom.

I'd been standing on the beach. It was empty. No people, no sea gulls, not even any shells on the long stretch of pale sand. And way far away, near the horizon that separated the pale sand from a white sky, there'd been a person. And that person had been walking away, getting smaller and smaller as I watched. I lifted my hand, trying to get the person's attention. But the person didn't seem to see me. When I tried to call, all that came out of my mouth was a whisper. The person kept getting smaller and smaller, then disappeared, and there was nothing but the sand and the white sky.

I lay quiet for a long time, feeling one hot tear after another slide out of my eyes. Finally I got up. I went over to the dresser, pulled open the top drawer, took out Mom's two letters and carried them back to the bed. Crawling under the covers, I curled up, holding them close. Then I fell asleep again.

Chapter Nine

"Wendy, I'm sorry!" Marlo apologized before I got the chance.

"Oh, Marlo, me, too!"

"Still friends?" she asked.

"What do you think?" I said.

"Best friends?"

"Totally!"

We hugged each other. "I'm so dumb," I admitted.

"Me, too," she said.

"Face it," I said. "We both are."

Then we laughed together, and she said, "Come on, best friend, let's walk to school. You can give me all the juicy details of how you managed to put Stephanie in her place."

"You heard?"

"Are you kidding? Everyone knows. Now come on, spill."

So I told her about my run-in with Stephanie, which really hadn't been all that major, but I elaborated on it enough so it sounded just a teensy bit more exciting. Then

I had a nagging thought. Wasn't that what Stephanie always did—exaggerated to make a story more exciting? But I didn't think I was hurting anyone. Was I?

Well, I promised myself, if anyone else asked me what had happened, I'd just tell them I didn't want to talk about it. Promising myself that, I felt a little better. Somewhat.

Sitting in first-period class, I started thinking about Gary again.

It was Friday, the day before my so-called date shell hunting with Gary on Sand Crab Key. But from the not-so-subtle way he'd been acting toward me all week, as if he were hinting that he didn't really want to go, I was pretty sure that I could count on sleeping in Saturday morning. And that made me angry. Not the sleeping part, but the way he'd handled the whole thing. If he had decided he didn't want to go with me, he could have come right out and said so. I'm not dense. I would have understood.

And that's when I decided I had to find him and tell him exactly what I thought of him.

But I didn't see him all morning. And lunchtime wasn't any better. Because of double session we barely had time to stand in line in the lunchroom much less eat anything. And Friday was chili-dog day—Marlo was a real freak for chili dogs. Before I could protest, she dragged me into line.

I saw him just as we were leaving the line. But he was way across the room. I would have had to do the 440 to reach him, chili dripping all the way, just to say two words before we had to go to class. And I definitely wanted to say more than two words.

I finally got my chance right before last period. I had gone to my locker and was just closing it when Gary came up.

"Hi, Wendy," he said, leaning on the wall above my locker door. "I've been looking all over for you."

"Oh!" I narrowed my eyes, facing him. "Obviously not very hard."

"Huh?" His expression was so innocent I almost believed him. But not quite. "Really, Wendy," he insisted, "I checked everywhere."

"Uh-huh, really." I scowled in disbelief, then started to walk away, deciding maybe that he'd get the message.

But he grabbed my shoulder. "Wait, Wendy, please!"

"What?" I gave him a cold look.

He took a deep breath, and his face hardened. "Look"—he let go of my shoulder and ran his hand over his hair—"I know I haven't been Mr. Personality all week. But I've had something on my mind. So, if I said or did anything to make you angry at me—hey, well, I'm sorry."

As I stared at him, I suddenly realized how I must have seemed to Marlo for the past couple of weeks. I hadn't exactly been Ms. Personality myself. Yet, I'd been totally upset with her when she hadn't understood my feelings. And before Gary and I had actually met, I'd told myself I understood his feelings. Yet I was acting just the opposite. Still, if it was because of the girl in California, I wasn't going to be all that understanding.

"OK," I said, shrugging slightly.

"So, then," he said shoving both hands into the front pockets of his jeans and hunching his shoulders, "you still want to go to that island tomorrow? You know, to look for shells?"

"Sand Crab Key?" I asked, trying to sound as if I were having a hard time remembering exactly what plans we'd made.

"Uh, yeah! That was the name."

"Ummm." I still wasn't smiling, but I managed to look a little more friendly. "I guess so."

"Great! Listen, I checked with my father, and there's no problem getting the car. So I can pick you up anytime you say."

"Well, we really should go early," I suggested. "Low tide is around four-thirty, so everyone who's into shell hunting gets there as soon as the sun comes up. Which means we should, too. Or all the good shells will already be picked over." I shifted my books in my arms, and as I did, the hand on the hall clock caught my eye. The bell was going to ring any second. "Gee, Gary, I've got to go. I don't dare be late to my next class. But about the time, how about five? Is that OK?"

"Five?" He nodded. "Sure—OK, great."

I started to back away. I thought for a second, then added, "And I'll bring lunch."

"Fantastic!" He grinned. I suddenly got that warm sensation in the pit of my stomach. "Make tuna sandwiches," he called. "They're my favorite."

"Well, I'll think about it," I said and grinned. Then I turned and hurried down the hall, mentally making a note to myself to pick up some canned tuna on the way home from school.

Chapter Ten

The sky behind us was a bright neon pink as we drove across the causeway to Sand Crab Key. Pulling into the parking lot that ran parallel to the beach, I noticed there were only three other cars so far. It was still early. Out along the edge of the surf, two people walked along, their heads bent as they searched for newly beached shells.

We unloaded our stuff and carried it out onto the sand. As Gary put down the cooler and the plaid blanket, he turned and gestured dramatically toward where the sun was slivering up over the horizon. "Behold!" his voice was solemn. "Red sky in the morning, sailor take warning. Do you know what that means?"

For a moment I wasn't sure just how to react. But then I giggled. I couldn't help it. He was so handsome and funny. Dropping my tote and the picnic basket I'd been carrying, I said, "If I were a sailor, and this were a ship, not an island, and that sky were really red, not pink, I'd be worried enough to wish for some rain gear. But I don't even see any clouds."

"Do you always go around wrecking people's dramatic moments?" Gary demanded. "So, OK"—he broke into a grin—"I admit the sky's really pink. But I've always thought that was such a great saying that I wished I could find someone to say it to." He unzipped his warm-up jacket and pulled it off. "And you seemed like the perfect person to say it to."

"I guess I feel honored," I replied, grinning back. I started peeling off my jeans; my dark-green, one-piece bathing suit was underneath.

He'd unbuttoned his jeans and was hopping around on one foot, wrestling with pulling them off. "Then you don't think it's going to rain on our parade?"

Pulling my sweat shirt over my head, I said through the fabric, "Do you always talk in clichés?"

"Only when it's this early in the morning," he answered, standing in an easy position, his hands on his hips. He was wearing a red racing suit. "See, I find it's easier to talk in clumps of words when I'm not really awake yet. That way people think I'm semi-intelligent."

I shook my head and laughed. "I never thought about it that way. So you aren't awake yet?" I said, eyeing the still cold-looking, grayish-green Gulf. "I think I know how to help you wake up." And before he had a chance to say anything, I turned and raced down to the edge of the surf, dipped my cupped hands in and raced back, slinging the water at him from a couple of feet away. It splashed wonderfully, all over the front of his chest.

"Yeeeoow," he yelled, leaping into the air. "Hey, that's cold!"

"I know," I said, giggling. "That's the idea. Are you awake now?"

"*Yes!*" he yelled. Then I noticed there was a wicked smile forming on his lips. He started toward me. I tried to back away. But I wasn't fast enough. Before I knew what was really happening, he'd scooped me up in his arms and was walking straight for the water.

"*No!*" I screamed.

"*Yes!*" he muttered through even white teeth.

"*Oh, no!*" I kicked my feet.

"*Oh, yes!*" He held me tighter.

Then I hit the water with a splash. He'd been right. It was cold—it was freezing! I screamed and stood up, then sputtered, "I'll get you." But he was already running down the sand, laughing over his shoulder.

I took after him. I'm a fast runner. I don't jog for nothing. But I wouldn't have caught him if he hadn't stumbled over a pile of seaweed that he hadn't seen because he was still laughing at me. I grabbed his arm at the same time, and we fell into a jumbled heap in the surf.

The tide was just going out, and as the sand slid out from underneath us, we grabbed at each other to keep from being pulled with it. Then a new wave came lapping in, swishing softly around us. I was suddenly very conscious of the odd mixture of cold water and Gary's warm arms, which were still wrapped around me. When I looked up, all I could see was his face. His eyes were very green.

"I—I think we'd better start looking for shells," I said. My voice sounded shaky, and I hoped Gary would think it was only because the water was cold.

"You're right," he answered. But I noticed it was a long moment before he took his arms away.

Walking back to the spot where we'd left our things, I had a strange feeling that he wanted to take my hand. But he didn't.

I suddenly tried to appear very busy, kneeling and going through my tote. "Do you have a collection bag?" I asked, keeping my eyes on the contents of the tote. "Because I brought an extra one just in case you didn't." I pulled out the two net bags and held one up.

"Thanks," he said, taking the bag. His voice sounded so normal that for a second, I wondered if I was the only one who'd felt something between us. Closing the tote bag, I stood up, being sure to put some distance between us.

Hooking the bag onto the band of his suit, Gary said, "I checked for one last night. But I must've packed all of mine in the stuff that went in the moving van."

I nodded. "Would you rather go alone or together?" I asked. The question was a normal one. Serious shell collecting is not considered a herd activity. Some people get very edgy when other people are looking in the same place. I'm one of the edgy kind. And because of that, and because of what had just happened, I hoped he would feel the same way.

"Please don't consider me antisocial," Gary said, "but I like to be alone when I'm shell hunting. I know I'm not familiar with the shells around here, but maybe I can just pick up what I think looks good, and you can tell me later if I've got any great finds."

"Sounds good to me," I answered, pretending to straighten out a snarl in the net bag I was holding. "I'm the same way." I gestured down at my tote. "I brought a paperback book on Florida shells if you want to check on something you find."

"Hey, thanks," he said. "That was thoughtful."

"Sure." I shrugged slightly and smiled up at him.

"Well, OK." He looked up and down the

beach. "Which direction do you want, north or south?"

"You choose," I said.

"North, then." He grinned and tapped me lightly on the shoulder. "Good hunting!"

When he turned his back, I put my hand up to the spot, sure that I could feel the warmth of his fingers still on my skin. I waited until he was at the water's edge before turning to go my own way.

The sun was getting hot on my shoulders as I hunched down beside a particularly excellent pile of shells. My collection bag was about full, and I saw what was the tail end of a Sozon's cone. It was a shell that I'd been searching for for a long time. I held my breath as I reached out and pulled it from the little pile of fragments where it was hiding. I smiled when I saw it was in good shape. But holding it closer to examine it, I sighed. It was only an extra-large alphabet cone.

The two shells are very much alike in that they are basically the same soft cream color. But the Sozon's is oranger with white-spotted bands; whereas the alphabet shell is white with orange and brown blotches.

I was putting it back for someone else to find, but then I paused. Maybe Gary would like it. I put it back in my bag.

Later, we sat cross-legged on the blanket, our two piles of shells between us. Gary had found some really good shells. But I noticed an alphabet cone wasn't one of them. I hesitated, then took the one I'd found out from under my knee where I'd put it, waiting to see if he'd found one of his own. I held it out.

"Maybe you'd like this one, too," I said. "The markings are particularly good." He took it, balancing it on his hand, examining it. "I know you said you only like to keep the shells you actually find yourself," I said. "But I thought that maybe you'd like to have this one for a while. You know until you find one on your own."

"It's really nice," he said, not looking up, but still turning the shell over in his hand. "It's an alphabet cone, isn't it?" That's when he looked up and smiled.

"Uh-huh." I nodded, smiling back.

"Thanks." He glanced back down at the shell, rubbing his thumb softly over the surface. "Really—thanks." The way he said it made me glad that I'd decided to save it for him. And watching him, I got that sudden, wonderful, warm feeling again. It was turning out to be a great day.

"Hey!" He lifted his head, giving me a lopsided grin. "Did you make those tuna sandwiches? I'm totally starved."

Gary dug into the plastic container and took the last brownie. Biting into it he groaned appreciatively. "Mmmm—man!

These are positively fantastic. Did you really make them yourself?"

"With these very hands," I said, holding up my hands and wiggling my fingers. "And," I confessed, "a box of mix."

Gary nodded seriously. "But you had to add eggs or something?"

"Eggs," I said. I was about to break out laughing.

"Be serious!" Gary admonished. "Ah, I have it! You have a genius for selecting the perfect eggs. Right?"

"Oh, right!" I agreed, then laughed because I couldn't help myself. Smiling, I put my head down on my hunched-up knees and looked over at him. He lay on his side, his head propped on one hand.

"You should be a member of the Florida Chamber of Commerce. You almost make me like it here," he said suddenly.

Thanks," I replied. "But don't give me too many compliments. I can only handle so many a day."

"OK, I'll remember." Gary grinned. "Two is your limit." Rolling over, he laid his head on his arms.

"What's California like?" I asked, really wanting to know.

"Oh, it's great," Gary answered. He turned his head so he could study me. "Funny! California and Florida have a lot in common. You know, beaches, lots of sun, orange trees, palms. But the two are so completely different." He thought for a second. "Florida's so flat. I guess that's maybe one thing I can't get used to. California has mountains. When you look out at the horizon, you see something besides just sky and the tops of palm trees."

"Sure," I said. "You see smog."

"I take back what I said about you. That was definitely an unkind remark."

"I'm defending Florida," I insisted.

"All right," he said and smiled. "I'll give you that. "But"— he motioned with his head toward the water—"look at that! Those aren't real waves. You can't surf on those things."

"Well, you can swim," I said. "Listen, do you scuba dive?"

"Yes, sure."

"OK," I argued. "Well, we've got these great places for diving. We even have an underwater park for divers only."

"Hey, I've heard about that place," Gary said with enthusiasm, sitting up. "In fact, I think I saw an article in some sports magazine about it. There were these photos of people following markers along an underwater trail." He shook his head. "Boy, I wish I could visit that place before I—" He suddenly broke off, turning away.

I stared at the back of his head, drawing my lower lip between my teeth. I felt as if someone had just dumped a bucket of cold water over me. I was positive I knew what Gary had been about to say when he'd stopped himself. He'd almost let slip that he was going to stay in California when he flew back there with his father during Easter vacation, that he didn't plan to come back. That's why he wouldn't be visiting any underwater park, at least not in Florida.

And that meant he was still interested in that girl in California. That's what it had to mean. And he'd really come on this trip because he wanted to collect shells. That was all. I was just the person who'd been handy to make him his tuna sandwiches—and the brownies.

Well, I wasn't going to let him know that I knew what he was thinking. Making my voice sound casual, but interested, I said, "What about the other places you've lived? I guess it must be exciting moving around, right?"

He didn't answer right away, just kept staring out at the water.

I sighed, ready to start putting my stuff together so we could leave, when he looked back at me, with a smile and a shrug and said "Yeah, we've definitely moved around a lot. Let's see. We've lived in Ohio, Virginia, Texas—I really don't like that state—New Mexico, and Nevada."

"What's wrong with Texas?"

"It stunk!" He made a face. "Oh, I guess that's not really fair. I don't know about the rest of the place. But this little town where we lived for a while was right in the middle of some oil fields, and they'd have these gas attacks, like smog attacks, but you couldn't believe the smell. And you couldn't get away from it. I mean you could go stand in the middle of a shower in your closed bathroom, and the smell would still find you." He shook his head. "I think that was the first time I was really glad to leave someplace." He grimaced again, remembering. Then he said, "What about you? Where else have you lived?"

"Nowhere, I've lived here all my life."

"Well, but you'll be leaving pretty soon, won't you? Samantha mentioned something about your mother having a new job in Philadelphia. So, you'll be moving there, right?"

"No." I shook my head again. "I'll be staying with my aunt." The sentence was easy, straightforward. But I guess my voice sounded a little bit strangled. Gary gave me a funny look.

"Is there some special reason why you're staying here instead of going to live with your mother?" Gary was studying me. "Is there some special guy?"

I shook my head. "I don't have a steady boyfriend." I looked down at my toes so that I wouldn't have to look him in the eye. I hugged my knees tightly. I certainly wasn't about to tell him that it had been solely my mother's decision for me to stay in Florida. That she'd just packed up and left me.

"Hey, look, Wendy," Gary said, and all at once he was apologetic, "I didn't mean to pry."

"That's OK. Anyway, you weren't really prying," I said, still staring at my toes. "We were just talking—asking questions about each other. I asked you questions, too. I didn't think I was prying."

I shut up then. And he didn't say anything, either. We were silent for a while. A trickle of perspiration ran down the back of my neck. The day was beginning to feel muggy. I raised my head and looked out at the Gulf. Some clouds had clumped themselves together and were playing tag with the sun, casting shadows on the surface of the water. I noticed there were some more clouds overhead. They were dark, and I thought about how Gary had kidded around about the red sky and the possibility of rain.

"How about your father?" Gary interrupted. "If you aren't going to live with your mother, why don't you live with him?"

"My father?" I repeated.

"Yeah," he gave me a quizzical look. "You know, the opposite of your mother. Does he live around here?"

"No." I shook my head.

"Well, where does he live?" It was a simple, curious question.

"My father doesn't live anywhere," I

answered. I could feel my throat begin to tighten, the way it always did whenever I thought about Daddy. I took a deep breath to make it stop. I forced myself to smile in a nonpersonal way. "My father's dead."

"Oh, geez!" Gary clapped his hand to his head. "Listen, Wendy, I'm sorry. I wouldn't have kidded around like that if I'd known. I'm really sorry."

"It's OK," I said. "I know you didn't know. I understand. But please don't say you're sorry. I hate it when people say they're sorry. It seems like such a dumb word when you say it about someone being dead."

"Right." He nodded. "I'm sor—OK."

I tried to quit making everything so serious. I didn't want to be serious. I wanted to go back to the way we'd been when we had eaten the picnic. Instead, I found myself squeezing my hands together and telling him about my father. "It happened out there," I said, my voice low. "In the Gulf. He was out in a boat, alone. He was a marine biologist, and he'd gone out to get some samples for an experiment he was working on. It was a nice day. I remember my mother taking me over to the park because there was one of those traveling carnivals there. I got cotton candy. When we got home, there was a station wagon parked in front of our house with the Coast Guard emblem on the door. They talked to my mother. I saw her start to cry, but then she stopped. The men drove away—" I stopped talking and swallowed hard. "There'd been some kind of explosion." I swallowed again. "They found a lot of wreckage—but they never found my father."

"I'm—" Gary started to say, then stopped. Instead, he reached out and put his hand over mine.

I kept staring out at the gulf. There were tiny whitecaps now, and the day didn't look so nice anymore. It was beginning to rain. I hoped Gary wouldn't notice that I had started to cry.

"Rain," Gary said. "It's starting to rain." Then it really came down—hard. Gary pulled me up. Gathering up the blanket, he piled it on top of the cooler. He picked up my tote and the picnic basket and handed them to me. Then he scooped up everything else. We ran toward the parking lot.

We were soaked by the time we reached the car. Gary had to fiddle with the lock for a few seconds. Then we both slid, dripping, into the front seat, slinging our stuff into the back.

For a minute we just sat there, panting. The car windows were fogging up. I could feel the cold water sliding off the ends of my hair, and I knew I must look awful. Gary's hair was plastered across his forehead. When he pushed it back, water ran down the sides of his face and neck and onto his chest. We looked at each other and started laughing at the same time.

"You look terrible," I managed to get out.

"You don't look so great, yourself." Then all at once he stopped laughing and leaned toward me, putting his lips softly on mine.

Chapter Eleven

It was still raining. It slid down the outside of my bedroom window, like an inside-out water-fall. Shoving my hands into the pockets of my yellow, quilted robe, I leaned against the sill and stared out at Aunt Eva's backyard. What I could see of it. It was like looking through the bottom of a very thick drinking glass. The orange and grapefruit trees wavered and curled each time a new sheet of water attacked the window.

Every time it rained Aunt Eva said that it was coming down in buckets. That's a dumb thing to say, I know. But actually, it pretty much describes Florida rain. There were times that I felt as if I were at the bottom of a swimming pool, and I wanted to push myself up to the surface to get a breath of air.

And if the rain kept up for an extralong time, the streets would flood for several hours. That's because Florida's coast areas are mostly sand.

Usually at that point, Marlo would get her

brother's inflatable raft out of the garage and paddle over to get me. Then we'd paddle around and visit everyone else. It was safe because it was too deep for cars to get around without stalling, so everyone just parked and waited it out. Those days it was fun. But this wasn't one of them—it was just gray and absolutely gloomy.

OK, I told myself, maybe it was actually good that I couldn't go jogging. Because I wasn't too sure how I would handle meeting Gary out on the beach. I was still confused about the kiss he'd given me in the car at Sand Crab Key.

I put my fingers to my mouth. I'd never really been kissed that way before. Well, I'd been kissed, but no kiss had ever sent the little electric currents racing up and down my back the way that kiss had. I closed my eyes and listened to the rain, remembering exactly how it had been in the front seat of his car. The rain had drummed on the roof and slid down the outside of the windows, just as it was doing outside this window.

I opened my eyes, staring into the backyard again. What was Gary doing now? Was he sleeping? Or was he sitting in Marlo's house eating breakfast? What did he like for breakfast? He couldn't be out jogging in this weather. Maybe he was looking out at the rain just as I was doing and thinking of me. My heart did a quick spin.

Could he be?

Or was he thinking about the girl in California?

That's where I got confused. How could Gary have kissed me the way he had if he still was in love with someone else?

I remembered how his sister had said Gary's personality was composed of a lot of layers that sheltered the real Gary. I thought I'd gotten through to him the day before, really understood him for the first time.

He did have a great sense of humor. Just as Samantha had said, it was a sort of one-on-one thing. I smiled to myself as I thought about throwing water all over him and his picking me up and carrying me down to dump me in the shallow waves. The picture of the two of us lying in the surf together raised a row of prickles down my back again, and I hugged myself. The prickles made me feel warm all over.

He was sensitive and understanding, too. I could tell that from the way he'd reacted when I'd talked about my father. I usually never did. Because when I did, most people got funny looks as if they wished I hadn't brought up the subject. Like death was something so obscene that you shouldn't mention it in polite company. But Gary hadn't been that way at all. His reactions had been honest, not phony and embarrassed.

So I knew he was honest.

But that's the part where I got confused. When we'd been comparing California and Florida, he'd suddenly broken off the conversation and started staring out at the water. What else could he have been thinking about but that girl in California?

So how could he have been thinking of her one minute, then kissing me the way he had the next? Suddenly I wasn't sure Gary was being honest at all.

A knock on the door made me jump. "Come in." I felt silly at having been caught daydreaming.

"Hi, Wendy, honey!" Aunt Eva cheerfully walked into the room. "Isn't this just the most horrible weather? I swear, it's coming down in buckets."

"Hi, Aunt Eva." I smiled at hearing the "buckets" again. I noticed she was dressed up in a beige pantsuit with a white silk and lace shirt. She looked very pretty. Her hair was brushed into a soft, shining blond halo. I felt positively scrungy. I hadn't even bothered to brush my hair yet.

"Honey," she said, "I came in to tell you that I have to go out for a little while."

"Out?" I scowled. "In this weather? How come?"

"Oh, one of those social things. You know how it is. Some friends of mine are having a brunch for some friends of theirs who are about to take off on an around-the-world cruise." She thought a minute. "Can you believe anyone these days having that much money?"

"Can you drive OK?" I asked.

"Sure!" Aunt Eva said. "My new little car doesn't stall the way that huge old heap used to. And I'll just avoid the worst intersections. Don't worry." She smiled to let me know I shouldn't be concerned. "But the reason I came in, besides letting you know I'd be gone for a while, was to tell you that I picked up some of those blueberry muffins you like, and they're in the breadbox. Also, I've squeezed some fresh orange juice, and that's in the refrigerator." She paused. "If you get really hungry, there's always bacon and eggs, too."

"Thanks," I said, laughing.

"Well, OK, honey." She smiled at me again. "Then I'll just be on my way. I'm only sorry that I have to leave you on such a dreary morning. It would be more fun to stay here and have breakfast with you and share the Sunday paper." She turned and put her hand on the doorknob. "But I won't be too long. I promise."

"Just be careful." Suddenly I felt very protective. I wanted to be sure she wasn't going to get hurt or stuck someplace.

"I will." She blew me a kiss, then closed the door softly behind her.

I heard her back the car out and went to

the window to watch her drive up the wet street.

All at once the house was very empty and silent. I felt as if I had to do something to make some noise. Breakfast seemed like the best thing.

Out in the kitchen I put one of the blueberry muffins into a microwave to heat, then got out the orange juice and poured some into a glass.

I finished the last of my muffin at the same time as I flipped shut the last page of the Sunday supplement. I'd tried to read some dumb article on brown pelicans, but I couldn't get past the third paragraph. Sunday papers were so boring, I thought, tons and tons of articles on stuff I never wanted to read about. I took my dirty dishes over and stacked them in the dishwasher. *What now?* I thought.

I wandered back through the living room. There was TV, but that's never very good on Sunday morning, either. Besides, without Aunt Eva, the living room seemed cold and unfriendly with all that delicate white wood and white brocade.

Glancing at the French provincial phone on the end table I thought about calling Marlo, but Marlo didn't believe in opening her eyes before noon on Sundays. And there was always the chance that Gary might answer the phone. It wasn't too likely, considering there were so many people currently living in the

Williamses' house. But, with my luck, he'd be the one who answered. Then what would I say? He'd probably think I was calling just to talk to him. No, that was a dumb idea. I wouldn't call.

I ended up back in my room, standing in front of the dresser, glaring at myself in the mirror. I was a mess. My hair was a total wreck.

The rain was still pouring down, heavy and gray, and it made me sad. Maybe that's why I started thinking about Mom. She'd never called back after that call on Thursday.

I scowled. Maybe she had called. Maybe Aunt Eva was out, or maybe I was in school.

All of a sudden I found myself opening the top drawer and digging through it for her letters, then walking back to the bed with them. Sitting down and pushing the pillows up behind me, I slowly turned the first letter over and opened the flap. I pulled out the folded sheets of paper and began to read.

I was halfway through the letter before I realized Mom hadn't written anything at all about what had happened before she'd left for up north. And nothing about her job. What she'd written about was Philadelphia—she'd written all about the city. There were descriptions of the famous landmarks, of little neighborhood parks, of a shopping mall, and a restaurant that served thirty-three different kinds of omelets. I frowned at first, wondering why she was taking so much space to tell me about a city I wasn't ever going to see. But, after the first page, I kept on reading because I really wanted to. The way she wrote, she made Philadelphia sound pretty and interesting. I was almost sorry when I got to the last page.

I was so into the second letter that I wasn't prepared for the last line when I read it. "I miss you very much, Dede." *Dede.* That was the nickname she and Daddy used to call me. I hadn't thought about it for a long time because she'd stopped calling me it the night after Daddy died.

I sat scrunched up against the pillows with the pages of her letter in my hand. I no longer saw them. Instead, I saw the little blue house with the white shutters on Dolphin Way, where we used to live. Mom hadn't been working then. She had painted. Her paintings of seashells had hung all over the walls of our house, and Daddy had hung some on the walls of his office at the university. She'd also taught me how to make a chocolate cake from scratch. And she'd been my troop's leader when I was in the Girl Scouts in sixth grade.

I looked down at the letter in my hand again. Very slowly and carefully I refolded it, putting it back in the envelope. Then I reached over, opened the drawer in the bedside table, and pushed through the things in it until I found what I was looking for, the box of stationery Marlo had given me for Christmas.

Pulling my knees up, I leaned back against the pillows and took out one of the sheets of stationery, settling it on top of the lid of the box. The stationery was light pink with a border of red hearts. I picked up my pen and began writing.

Chapter Twelve

"Are we still going to the drive-in tonight?" Samantha asked, squiggling her sunscreen over her leg and smoothing it into her skin.

"Of course," Marlo replied, flopping over onto her stomach and leaning on her elbows. "I've been wanting to see that horror movie for absolutely ages."

It was Friday afternoon, and the three of us were lying on our towels near The Hut. Some of the kids were playing volleyball, and we were watching them.

"What are you going to wear, Wendy?" Marlo turned her head to look at me.

"Oh, I don't think I'll go," I said, trying to make my voice sound as casual as possible. I looked up and saw Gary. He was standing up near the net. Just at that moment, he looked over and smiled. I smiled back, then looked down and pretended to brush some sand off my towel.

"Why not?" Marlo demanded. "This morning you said you'd go. Now what's wrong?"

107

"Nothing. I have some things to do, that's all."

"Oh, come on, that's a dumb reason. What things?" Marlo made a face. "I don't believe you. You just don't want to go because you think it's beginning to sound like a date."

"That's not it," I insisted. "Really! I've got some stuff to do."

"Sure!" Samantha made a face, too. "Look, it just so happens that there's the six of us—you, me, Marlo, Andy, Roger, and Gary. We're all just going to a movie. I know Andy and Marlo are dating and Roger and I are dating, but so what? You can go with Gary without it being a date. It's just the way it works out."

"Then Gary won't mind if I'm not there," I said.

"Will you stop being ridiculous!" Marlo insisted. "So, what are you going to do after you do all this stuff you say you have to do, sit and stare at TV? Or maybe go to bed?"

"But a drive-in?" I shook my head emphatically. "No!"

"It's not going to be like that," Samantha argued, putting the sunscreen on her other leg. "We're taking Andy's pickup and putting the cushions from the outdoor furniture in the back. Then when we get to the movie, we'll all sit together. No one's going to be fooling around. It'll be too crowded for that, anyway. Besides, I really want to see this movie." She poked Wendy. "Don't you Wendy? I mean, it's a great horror movie."

I shrugged. "Maybe."

"Look," Marlo said, taking up the argument, "we're going to make popcorn and put soft drinks in the cooler. Everything. And it won't be fun if you don't come. Say you will! Listen, I won't take no for an answer."

"Oh, OK," I said reluctantly. Inside I was still telling myself I shouldn't.

"Great!" Marlo said and grinned. "Now that's settled." She turned to Samantha. "I've been dying to ask you something. *What's* happened to your brother? I mean all at once he's acting positively friendly, and last week he was walking around like someone had just told him he had only three days to live." She made a face. "If he were still acting that way I wouldn't blame Wendy for not wanting to go to the movies with him. But look at him!" Marlo gestured toward the volleyball game. "He walks and talks and laughs and smiles like everyone else."

"I know what you mean," Samantha said. "He's acting like himself again. I only hope it means he's decided to stay here." She grimaced. "Easter vacation is next week. And you know what that means."

"Yeah," Marlo agreed, "that stupid idea. Cutting out on your father when they get to California. Do you think maybe that's why he's acting the way he is? That he's still thinking of doing that, and it's just getting closer to the time to leave?"

"I don't know." Samantha looked unhappy. "But he hasn't said anything else to me about it, so it's possible he's decided to forget it and just go for the visit, the way Dad thinks he is."

"What do you think, Wendy?" Marlo asked.

"Me?" I shrugged, trying to appear casual. "I don't know." But the minute she'd asked me, my heart suddenly had started thumping against my ribs. "I guess I haven't really been paying all that much attention," I lied.

"What do you mean?" Marlo frowned. "I saw the two of you standing in the hall laughing together yesterday. That, dear Wendy, is definitely what I call paying attention."

"Really," I said lamely. "We just happened to be laughing at something funny that we both saw at the same time. That's all."

"Sure!" Marlo leaned toward me, her eyes narrowed. "Talk about people acting weird. Is it catching?" Then she rolled her eyes before settling back on her towel. "Well, personally," she said, talking to Samantha again, "I think Gary's just finally beginning to like Florida."

"I honestly hope you're right," Samantha said. "But I—"

There was a shout from the direction of the volleyball game. We all glanced over just in time to see Roger make a terrific spike.

"Oh, he's so fantastic, isn't he?" Samantha said with a sigh. Then she realized what she'd said and looked at Marlo and me and blushed. "Well, I mean he *is* cute. Isn't he?"

Marlo and I turned and looked at each other, and we both said at the same time, "Whatever you say!"

"Oh, forget it," Samantha mumbled. Then she pretended to be involved with her elbow, sticking it out for us to see, "Look, I think I've finally stopped peeling."

"Um-hmmm," Marlo said, tossing her head and giving me a "we know" look. "Hey!" Marlo suddenly leaned toward Samantha and pointed at the thin gold chain around Samantha's neck. "Is that new?"

"I thought you'd never notice," Samantha said, blushing.

"It's pretty," Marlo said.

"When did you get it?" I asked.

"Oh, last night." She ran her fingers back and forth over it. "Roger gave it to me."

"Roger?" Marlo said.

"You mean *the* Roger you just said was darling? Our Roger?"

"Fantastic," Marlo corrected me. "She said he was fantastic."

"Uh-huh. He asked me to be his girl-friend."

"Why didn't you tell us before this?" I demanded.

Marlo and I looked at each other for a second, then screamed, "Congratulations!"

Samantha just sat there grinning and looking shy but happy.

"Listen, we've got to go celebrate." Marlo took Samantha's arm and pulled her to her feet. "Come on! You can tell us every detail over Cokes."

Just as we were heading across the sand in the direction of The Hut, Andy and Roger and Gary came loping up. "Hey," Andy called, "where're you going?"

"We're celebrating Samantha's chain," Marlo announced.

"What chain?" Andy asked.

I noticed Roger turn red, then he recovered and put his arm around Samantha's shoulders. "I thought it was about time I *chained* her up," he said.

There was a chorus of groans. Then Andy said, "Did I hear someone offer to buy Cokes?"

I don't remember what we all talked about while we drank our Cokes. But I do remember that Gary and I somehow ended up on the same bench, and I was very aware of the fact that his leg was touching mine. At one point I nearly spilled my drink, but Gary caught the cup before it fell over. When he handed it back, our hands accidentally touched.

He smiled at me. It seemed a very personal smile. I smiled back but then turned toward

112

one of the others, pretending to be interested in whatever it was they'd just said.

Maybe it was my turn to draw back from our relationship. Or whatever you'd call what there was between Gary and me. For the past week he had been open and friendly. But all I could think of was that it was getting closer and closer to Easter vacation and that he hadn't mentioned any change of plans to his sister. Which to me meant he still intended to return to the girl in California.

Yet, whenever he looked at me or whenever something happened, like his touching my hand just then, I couldn't help but feel that I was beginning to mean something to him.

Or was I only kidding myself? I didn't know.

When we'd all finished our drinks, Roger and Samantha went walking down the beach holding hands. Andy gave Gary a friendly punch and challenged him to a one-on-one game. And Marlo and I went back to where we'd left our towels.

"OK, Wendy," Marlo started in as soon as we'd settled down on our towels, "confess!"

"Huh?" I looked blankly at her.

"I know I'm dense. It took me all this time to figure it out. But why didn't you tell me?"

"Tell you what?"

"About Gary, of course. It was fairly obvious, the way you were acting over there."

"I really don't know what you're talking about."

"Come on, Wendy," Marlo pleaded. "It's me—Marlo Williams—your best friend." She shook her head. "Something happened when you two went to that place—what's the name?—to hunt for shells. I never figured there'd be romance involved. Oh, wow!" She looked almost stunned.

I bit my lip, not saying anything.

"You really like him, don't you? No wonder you've been acting slightly weird. And no wonder he's been acting so happy. That is it, isn't it? He likes you, too?"

I didn't say anything for a second. Then I answered in a small voice, "I don't know."

So then, how come you didn't want to go to the drive-in tonight? You two could be together." Marlo sounded confused.

"Because I don't know," I said.

"Because you don't know what?" Her face mirrored her confusion.

"Because *I don't know* how he feels about me."

"Oh, yeah, the girl in California," Marlo said. "I'd almost forgotten about her." Then suddenly she grinned. "I bet he has, too." She thought a minute. "Sure, I bet he has."

"But we don't really know," I insisted. "And I'm not the kind of person who tries to steal another person's boyfriend, even if she is three thousand miles away."

"Yeah," Marlo agreed. "I know you're not, Wendy. But then, what are you going to do?"

I shrugged.

"All right," Marlo said, leaning on her knees, "let's think about this." She frowned. "You've really got to find out for sure about that girl. It's dumb to just sit around and speculate."

"So, what am I supposed to do? Go up and ask him? 'Gary, tell me, are you still madly in love with your old girlfriend?' "

"Well, I would," Marlo said easily. "But I know you—you wouldn't. So I'll do it. I'll find out for you."

"How?" I suddenly panicked, knowing Marlo's penchant for being open—sometimes too open—about everything.

"Oh, don't sweat it!" she said, putting a hand on my arm. I won't do anything to embarrass you. I promise."

"Then how do you propose to find out?"

"I propose, my dear best friend, to do a little bit of snooping. I plan to raid his dresser drawers. I am going to—"

"Hey, wait!" It was my turn to grab her arm. "You're not going to read those letters from his girlfriend, are you? I mean that's against the law. And it's wrong besides. Anyway, I don't want to know what she wrote."

"Cool it!" Marlo assured me. "I wouldn't do anything illegal." She hesitated. "But I wouldn't mind doing something just this side

115

of that." She pouted prettily. "Anyway, wouldn't you do the same for me—your best friend?"

"I guess. . . ." I grinned.

"OK, then." She grinned back. "And don't worry. I'll be just like the Pink Panther. He'll never know I was there."

Chapter Thirteen

"I want some pizza," Marlo declared. "Come on, Wendy, come with me while I get it." She gave me one of those heavy looks that meant "I've got to talk to you alone." Then she began to climb over the tailgate of the pickup, pulling me along with her.

"What the heck do you want pizza for?" Andy complained. "We've got a ton of popcorn, so what do you want with pizza?"

"Popcorn isn't the same thing as pizza," Marlo explained easily. "I just feel like pizza."

Andy knew there was nothing he could do. "All right. Just try and get back before the movie starts."

When we were several feet away from the truck, I turned to her and said, "OK, what is it?"

"Not here! Let's go to the girls' room. I want to check my hair, anyway."

"Nobody can hear us, and your hair looks great. Just tell me what it was you dragged me away to tell me. Because if you're not really

117

going to get pizza, I don't feel like struggling through that crowd just to watch you play with your hair."

"Oh, OK, but at least let's pretend we're going to the snack bar."

"Look, Marlo, if you want to talk, talk." I was losing my patience. "Come on, Marlo, tell me."

"Well," she said, drawing out the word, "I found out something about Gary that I think you'll like."

"You did?" I grabbed her shoulder. "Are you sure I'll like it?"

"Of course." She gave me an impish grin.

"Well, then what?" I started to shake her.

"OK—OK. Don't break my shoulder. It's simply that there's no trace of that girl in his room. I mean there's no longer any picture. And I couldn't find a single pink letter."

"Really?"

"Really!"

I let go of her shoulder. Then I had a thought, and I frowned. "Maybe you didn't check the right places. I mean, maybe he didn't want to put smelly stationery in with his clothes, so he hid the letters someplace else."

"No way!" Marlo shook her head. "I looked everywhere. Honest! Don't you think I couldn't find something smelling of Charlie, no matter where it was hidden?"

"Yeah." I nodded slowly. "OK, I think you're right. But—"

"Forget the buts, Wendy!" Marlo interrupted. "The bottom line is that he's gotten rid of the picture and the letters. And that means he's no longer interested in Miss California! Don't you get it? That means the field is now definitely clear. So go for it!"

"Are you sure you looked everywhere?" I insisted.

"What do you want, Wendy?" She hit her forehead with the palm of her hand. "A signed agreement? Look, will you get real, Wendy? Can't you see what's really happened? Gary likes you. That's why he's been acting the way he has all week. Even I can see that. So he decided to dump his old girlfriend. And that's it." She shook her head. "Sometimes I think you are so dense! Now come on. Let's go back. You have to get him to put his arm around you."

"OK, where's the pizza?" Andy demanded when we got back. "Don't tell me you guys ate it all."

"We decided not to get any," I told him as he helped us in.

"You're kidding?" he said. "What were you doing all this time? You've been gone for twenty minutes."

"We decided we didn't want oregano breath." Marlo winked at me. "Who wants to kiss a pepperoni?"

"Hey, the movie's starting." Roger and Samantha were snuggled up together against the back of the cab. "Throw us a couple of Cokes and sit down so we can see."

Andy put his arm around Marlo's waist and pulled her down beside him. He kissed the end of her nose, then bent over and got out Cokes for Samantha and Roger.

He glanced over at Gary and me. I was leaning casually against one side of the pickup. Gary was about two feet away. "You guys want Cokes too?" Andy asked.

I nodded. Andy threw us each a can and settled down beside Marlo.

All at once I was aware of the distance between Gary and me. It seemed more like two miles than two feet. I didn't think Gary's arm could reach.

Gary grinned at me. "How about some popcorn to go with the Coke?" He pulled back one of the sacks of homemade popcorn, putting it between us so that it filled up the space. "There," he said. "Now we can both get it."

"Great!" I smiled at him.

We ate the popcorn and concentrated on the movie. I was very careful not to put my hand into the sack at the same time that Gary did. I didn't want our hands accidentally meeting in the popcorn. That just didn't seem romantic.

The first movie was one of those really awful ones—this mad scientist puts a genius brain into a jar, then hooks the jar up to a computer and starts ruling the world.

At intermission Gary stood up to stretch, then sat down again. This time right beside me.

The second movie was really scary. This insane person went around in the middle of the night, hacking away at people with a meat cleaver. One part scared me so much I really screamed and buried my head in Gary's shoulder. Gary put his arm around me and said, "Don't worry. You're safe with me."

He kept his arm there, too, all the way home. It would have been perfect, if it hadn't been for one small thing. He didn't kiss me good night. He shook my hand.

Chapter Fourteen

"He shook your hand?" Marlo gasped. "I don't believe it! He honestly shook your hand?"

"Well"—I shifted the receiver to my other hand—"actually it was more like a squeeze than a shake, a friendly squeeze." I thought about it again. "Yes, it was definitely a friendly squeeze."

"Well, listen, Wendy." Marlo was trying to make me feel better. "That's not so bad—really! Maybe Gary's just the type who takes things slow. He'll probably kiss you the next time."

"But everything was so perfect," I complained. "He walked me to the door. It was dark. The front porch even smelled like orange blossoms. You can't ask for more than that. Besides," I went on, "it's not as if that would have been the first time. He's already—" I stopped talking.

"He's already what?" Marlo asked excitedly.

"Oh, well, he's already kissed me once," I admitted.

"You're kidding? And you didn't tell me? Where? When?"

"At Sand Crab Key," I said softly, remembering. "And that was in daylight. And I was wet, and we both looked drowned."

"Boy! It's worse than I thought. You've got it bad." She paused. "Darn it! I have to get off the phone. I've got to get ready. I don't even have my makeup on yet."

"You're going someplace? Where?"

"Wendy! I told you yesterday. Our family's taking the Vrieses to Epcot Center and Disney World for the weekend. We won't be back until late tomorrow night."

"Oh, rats. Well, have a good time."

"Oh, I will," Marlo said brightly. "You know Disney World is about my favorite place. I never get tired of going there. Tell you what, I'll ride Space Mountain with Gary for you."

"Oh, gee, thanks," I muttered.

"Look, Wendy," Marlo said in her best consoling voice, "we'll talk about this on Monday. OK? But I honestly don't think you have anything to really worry about. Like I said, I think Gary's the slow type. You have to give him time."

"I don't know if I have the time," I said anxiously. "Do you realize Easter vacation's less than one week away?"

"You have to give him time, or you'll lose

him completely. Look," Marlo insisted, "he didn't exactly look like he was in pain at the drive-in. I'm sure he likes you. Honest!" She paused. "Now, I've really got to go."

"OK," I grumbled.

"Be good," she said. "See you Monday."

Then I hung up. *A whole weekend to myself,* I thought. *What am I going to do to keep my mind off Gary?*

I started by helping Aunt Eva clean the house. Then she suggested we make fresh bread.

We ate practically the entire loaf, sitting at the kitchen table, butter melting onto our fingers. The rest of the weekend I spent doing my homework, jogging, and reading a new mystery from Aunt Eva's book club.

Monday morning I dressed very carefully in my purple designer jeans and a new lilac blouse my aunt had just given me. I ran into Gary that morning in the hall.

"Hi," I said with my biggest smile. "How'd you like Disney World?"

"Hey, it was terrific!" He gave me a friendly grin. I couldn't figure out if it was because he was still on a high from having a great weekend in Orlando or because he was glad to see me.

"You know it's almost like Disneyland in California. Just a few rides are different, that's all. I almost felt as if I were home again."

Gary stopped talking for a second. I think he must've realized that he'd mentioned California, where *she* was. "Sort of," he ended up lamely.

"So," I said, my voice still enthusiastic, "how'd you like Space Mountain? Marlo said she'd see that you rode it."

The haunted look that had come over his face for just a second had disappeared. "Wendy, it was great. Better than the Matterhorn. That's the ride that's kind of the same in—"

"I know," I said, cutting in. "Then you really had a great time, huh?"

"Yeah!" He glanced around as the late bell rang. "Hey! Better go. Catch you later. OK?"

"Right!" I smiled and wagged my head in a friendly way. But after he'd disappeared around the corner, I let my face slide into the worried expression that was a mirror of what was going on inside my head. I didn't care if those letters and that girl's picture weren't anywhere in his room. I had a horrible feeling they were still imprinted quite firmly inside his heart.

On Wednesday afternoon when we met briefly between classes, he was almost distant and that horrible feeling became much stronger.

On Thursday things were even worse. It was as if I had become invisible to Gary again. Something had happened, but what?

125

I found out at lunch. Coming up to the table in the cafeteria where Marlo and Samantha were sitting, I knew right away something was wrong.

Sliding into an empty chair, I said, "Hi, gang! OK, what's wrong?"

Samantha shook her head and continued to stare morosely at the melted cheese sandwich she was holding. There was one bite out of it. "Gary's actually going to go through with it. He's going back to California."

"Oh." My heart dropped like a stone, straight to the bottom of my stomach.

Without letting Samantha see her do it, Marlo gave me a sympathetic glance. "The girl in California sent him another letter. It came yesterday. You could smell the Charlie all the way from the mailbox."

"Yeah," Samantha said, looking up at me. "And Gary's been a walking zombie ever since. Haven't you noticed?" She took a bite of her sandwich, then frowned at it as if it had suddenly turned into something really horrible. She put it down. "I just wish I could think of a way to keep him from going."

"You mean like tying him up and pushing him in the nearest closet?" Marlo suggested.

"You've got it!" Samantha nodded.

"I don't understand," I said in a voice that was so low I was sure only I'd heard it. "She hasn't written since those first two letters. Why now?"

But Samantha heard. "*Why now* is right!" Her mouth turned down so hard there were little white patches under her bottom lip. "Why now?"

I was sitting in my bedroom on Friday afternoon, not reading, but turning the pages of a mystery, trying my best not to think about the fact that Gary was planning to fly out of my life forever.

For the third time I'd tried to focus on one particular paragraph when there was a knock on the door. It was Aunt Eva.

"Wendy," she said, poking her head around the side of the door, "there's someone out here to see you."

"Oh? Who?" I glanced up. Probably it was Marlo.

She raised her eyebrows in a way that was both a question and answer at the same time. "It's that good-looking young man who took you shelling out at Sand Crab Key. You know, the one who's staying at the Williamses'."

"Oh," I said again. I didn't trust my mouth to say anything else. My first thought was to tell Aunt Eva I didn't want to see him. I hate goodbyes. But then I told myself firmly that I wasn't being fair. Besides, what if Gary had come over to tell me he loved only me and that all he was doing was going to California for a visit with his father? My breathing got all confused at that thought, and I looked down in a panic at what I had on, ancient jeans and my comfortable at-home sweat shirt. Aunt Eva saw me.

"Why don't you just put on your pink sweat shirt and brush your hair," she suggested. "I'll tell him you'll be right out." Then she added with a twinkle, "I think he has a surprise for you. At least he has a very prettily wrapped package with him. And I can't imagine who else it would be for."

Then before I could ask her anything about that, she was gone.

My hands felt cold, and my heart started beating at my ribs, as if it wanted out. I changed into my pink sweat shirt, and then I brushed my hair and checked myself in the mirror. *Why is he here?* I asked my reflection. But my reflection didn't know any more than I did.

Entering the living room, I saw Gary sitting on the white couch. He was wearing tan slacks and a dark green polo shirt. The color of the shirt made his tan really stand out. His hair was more carefully combed than usual. I noticed the package Aunt Eva had mentioned. It was sitting on the couch beside him. It wasn't large, about the size of box that a piece of jewelry would come in, and it was wrapped neatly in silver paper with a dark blue satin ribbon. When he saw me, Gary stood up.

"Hi!" I said, trying to smile in a casual

way. But I suddenly realized I didn't know what to do with my hands.

"Hi, Wendy," he said, then sort of cleared his throat, as if he planned to say more. But he didn't.

After a second I said, "Would you like to sit down?"

"Uh, yes, thank you." He looked behind him. To see if the couch was still there, I thought. I wanted to tell him it hadn't moved. "How about you?"

"Sure." I nodded. "OK."

But I didn't know where to sit. If I sat in one of the little silk side chairs, it might seem as if I were trying to avoid being near him. And, after all, we had kissed in our bathing suits, and we had shared popcorn from one bag. So I walked over and sat on one end of the couch.

"How are you?"

"I'm fine," I said.

He suddenly scowled. I was reminded of that first day we'd met. And I almost started to do the same thing I'd done then, too, scowl back. But before I could, he picked up the wrapped package.

"Wendy!" The scowl marks lightened. "Wendy, uh, look, I'm not good at—"

"Yeah." I said and nodded, breaking in. "I know how that is."

Somehow I didn't want to hear whatever words he was trying to say. Because if they

129

weren't what I wanted to hear, I felt not hearing them wouldn't let them be true. At least not for a while. So I blurted out the first thing that landed on my tongue. "Samantha said you were going to California for the whole week. That's really terrific!" I smiled, pretending to be happy for him.

The scowl was back again. "Listen, Wendy"—he was holding the package toward me—"like I said, there are some things I'm not very good at expressing with words. So, well, I thought that this would do it better for me." He pushed the package into my hands. "Here!"

I took it. It wasn't very heavy. It almost felt as if there weren't anything inside at all.

"I hope you like it."

"Oh, I will."

"Well—look. Do me a favor and open it later, not now. OK?"

"OK." I nodded. It was kind of strange, his asking me that. I hadn't made a move to even untie the bow. "Thank you." I held up the box to examine it. "The paper's pretty."

"I'm glad—" he said. "Glad you like it."

Suddenly it was as if he couldn't stand to sit on the couch with me for another second. He looked at his watch, then leaped up. He checked his watch again. "Hey, I guess I'd better go. I've still got some packing to do, and we're catching a plane in Tampa at eight."

"Oh, sure." I stood up, too. "I know how it

is with last-minute packing," I lied. I couldn't remember if I'd ever last-minute-packed.

"Well," he said, edging toward the door, "take care." He nodded at the package, which was still in my hands. "I really do hope you like it. I mean, I hope you understand what it was I was trying to say with it."

I couldn't think of a right answer, so I just said, "You'd better get going. You don't want to miss that plane."

"Right—right!" For one last second he looked at me with those green, green eyes. Then he was out the door and walking quickly down the front walk.

Slowly I closed the door, then stood watching it for a long second as if he might come back if I waited long enough. Finally I took the package over to the couch and sat down. Very carefully I peeled away the ribbon and the wrapping. Beneath the silver paper was a white cardboard box, the sort of box jewelry might come in. But when I took off the lid, my breath caught in my throat. Resting on its protective bed of cotton was something far more precious than any piece of jewelry.

It was Gary's queen tegula shell.

Looking down at the perfect, pearly white ridges that swirled around the top of the shell, I was almost positive I understood the meaning of his gift.

Chapter Fifteen

It was Monday, Gary had been gone for three days and it seemed like three weeks. I couldn't get my mind off him. I kept wondering if he'd made up with the girl in California yet.

I was curled up on the chaise, staring out at the front lawn, watching an egret stalk around as if he owned the place. It was a beautiful day. The sky was full of puffy clouds drifting along over the tops of palms. It was a day that should have made anyone feel terrific. But not me. I was too busy having an I-feel-sorry-for-myself day. But I had every right to. First my mother had left for some new career she had considered more important than my happiness. Then the first boy I'd ever felt something important for left, too—for a girl who used perfume the way some people use bug spray. Why couldn't Gary see *I* was the perfect girl for him?

Then I remembered the queen tegula shell sitting in its cardboard box on top of my dresser. Gary *did* care about me. He cared enough to have given me something he prized, something that couldn't really be replaced. And Gary must have known I'd understand that.

But when he'd come over to say goodbye, I'd sat there like a complete jerk, telling him he'd better leave or he'd miss his plane. As if I couldn't get rid of him fast enough. Thinking about that made me want to slide down and hide under the chaise forever. Well, maybe I *wasn't* the perfect girl for Gary after all.

I sighed heavily and stared out at the egret again, just in time to see him fly gracefully away. "You, too!" I muttered.

Just as I was about to go down in misery for about the third time, the phone rang. Aunt Eva wasn't home, so I went out to answer it. It was Marlo.

"Hi!" she said breezily.

"Humph!" I grumped back.

"Hey, what's with you?" she asked, then, "Oh, I forgot. Look, will you stop moping around! I told you yesterday that, as far as everyone knows, Gary is still doing exactly as planned. He's seeing friends, and he and his father are both staying at a motel. Nothing's happened. Therefore, nothing may happen. OK?"

"But the week isn't over yet," I argued. "He may be waiting until just before his father leaves to tell him he isn't coming back here.

And about those friends, one of them has to be the Charlie girl. That I'm positive of!"

"Positive?" Marlo made a snorting sound. "Who made you Jeane Dixon?"

"Listen," I said, "I just know, that's all!"

"Oh, well," she said with a tiny sigh, "if you're going to insist on wallowing in self-pity all week, I'll just hang up. But I thought you'd like to go down to the beach with Samantha and me. The weather's great! Or haven't you bothered to notice?"

"I've noticed," I answered, halfway sounding sullen and halfway sounding friendly because she *had* called to ask me to come along. "But I can't."

"You can't, or you don't want to?"

"I really can't," I insisted. "My aunt sold a property today that she's been trying to sell for ages, and she's asked me to go out to lunch with her to celebrate. She's over at the escrow office right now, and she'll be back any second."

I glanced down at myself then, realizing I hadn't changed yet and was still wearing a pair of old shorts and a shirt with enough mustard stains to make it look like an abstract painting. "And I've got to go change right now before she gets here. So I'm going to hang up so you and Samantha can get going." I hesitated. "But thanks for calling to ask me to go with you. Honest!"

"Well, OK," she answered. "But I hope you

cheer up for your aunt. She doesn't deserve to have someone as depressing as you around to help her celebrate."

"Don't worry, I will," I assured her.

"I'll call you back later when we get back and you get back. OK?"

"OK."

"Smile!" she said as a final parting shot.

I hung up and a few seconds later the phone rang again. I picked it up, thinking, *Oh, Marlo, give it up!* But the voice wasn't Marlo's.

"Wendy, Wendy? Honey, is that you?"

"Mom?"

"Yes. Can you hear me all right?"

"Yes."

"It's so good to hear your voice again! I've missed you so much."

"Uh—" I swallowed hard. "I've missed you, too, Mom."

"Wendy, I have the letter you wrote me sitting here in front of me. I've read it over several times—thank you for writing."

"Well—uh—gee, it wasn't anything great," I said.

"When my daughter tells me she loves me," Mom said in a low, warm voice, "I consider that to be great."

There was a pause. I didn't know what to say next. Then Mom said, "Wendy, did my letters give you an idea of what Philadelphia's like?"

135

"Yeah, it sounds like a neat place."

"That's exactly what I think," Mom said, suddenly sounding suspiciously like an anxious salesperson. "The reason I wrote you all about Philadelphia is, well, I thought you might consider coming up here to spend the summer. You know, if you don't have anything else planned."

"Mom, ah—I don't know. That sounds great. But, well, could I have some time to think about it? I mean, summer's still kind of far away." My mind flew to thoughts of Gary. Would he be back? Was there really a chance he would be?

"But it isn't!" Mom insisted. "It's only a couple of months away. And I really want to know what you think about the idea. Oh, Wendy! There are so many places I want to show you. Just wait until you taste one of the omelets at The Egg Carton—"

"Mom, please. Let me think it over. Give me some time," I pleaded.

There was a pause, a long one. I closed my eyes. What did Mom really want?

"Well," Mom's voice was low when she continued, "I was thinking, too, that if you came up here this summer, you might find you like it so much that you'd decide to stay here for your senior year."

"Oh."

"Wendy?"

"Mom, I don't know." It was all much too

136

sudden. Couldn't she understand that? There was Gary; my friends; Aunt Eva—I had to think. It didn't seem possible that Mom was actually waiting on the other end of the line for me to make a decision like that.

"I'm sorry, honey," Mom said, breaking the silence. "I know I'm asking too much, too fast. But it's just that I want it so much. Do you understand? I know I've got to give you time to think about all this. But will you promise to think seriously about what I'm asking?"

I paused for a long time, then said, "Yes, Mom, I promise." Then I added, "Mom, I do love you!"

"Me, too, Wendy! Me, too," she said in a voice so low I could barely hear her.

I think we both hung up at the same time.

When Aunt Eva came back from the escrow office, I hadn't even changed. I was still sitting on the couch in my grungy shorts and old shirt. When she saw me, she came right over and sat down beside me, wanting to know what was wrong.

When I told her about Mom's phone call, she just looked at me for a minute, then put her hand softly on mine and said, "It sounds like a very hard decision to have to make."

I nodded. "I guess it's about the hardest decision I've ever had to consider in my entire life." I bit on my lower lip. "I'm not even sure I can make that kind of decision."

Aunt Eva's hand was still over mine. "You said your mother's suggestion was for you to visit during the summer, then think about staying permanently. That means you don't have to decide right away."

"I know. But I don't even know if I really want to stay with her for the summer. Mom makes Philadelphia sound like an exciting place. But I can't believe she really wants me with her. I can't forget the way it was when she left. She didn't bother to ask me to be with her then. She just wanted to go away by herself so she could have her new career and her new life. Without me."

"Oh, no—no—no!" Aunt Eva put both her arms around me and hugged me tight. "You mustn't think that, ever. Let me tell you something about your mother. You know, maybe you haven't noticed because you've been busy with your own life, but your mother hasn't been happy for quite a while. I think living here constantly reminded her of your father. If she didn't love you so very much, she wouldn't have stayed here as long as she did. She was trying to hang on because she knew this was your home."

"But I loved my father, too. I still do," I insisted. "And that's one of the reasons why I like being here. It reminds me of him, and I can think of him often. Sometimes it makes me sad, but mostly it makes me happy to remember him."

"That's exactly the way I feel, too. Remember, he was my brother, and I loved him, too." She patted my shoulder. "But we're all different, honey. And for your mother, the memories, the constant reminders, are too strong for her." She smiled a sad little smile. "We each have to handle our grief in our own way. And I think that's the real reason why your mother took the job in Philadelphia."

"But why didn't she tell me all of this?" I looked directly at Aunt Eva. "I would have understood."

"Would you?" Aunt Eva looked back at me. "I'm not so sure you would have then."

I really was beginning to understand a lot. But there was even more I wanted to think about—alone. "Aunt Eva," I said, "would you mind terribly if we celebrated your sale with dinner instead of lunch? I think I'd like to go down to the beach for a while."

"Of course," Aunt Eva said. I knew she understood.

I walked for a long time. I went in the opposite direction from The Grass Hut so I wouldn't run into Marlo or Samantha or any of my other friends. I really did need to be alone for a while in order to sort out my thoughts.

After I'd gone a couple of blocks down the beach, I realized I was walking toward the old wooden pier where Gary and I had had our first conversation—or argument—whichever.

I smiled to myself, thinking back on that night. I laughed a little at how much we'd each misunderstood. It was a night that I'd always remember.

But now it was daytime. The sun was overhead instead of a full moon. And Gary was more than three thousand miles away.

The pier was up ahead. It really wasn't a pier; it was more a relic that was waiting for the next big storm to dash it into the waves. Then it would be gone, too.

At the beach end of the pier, there was one solid post that slanted off to the side, making a good place to sit and lean against. For maybe half an hour I sat, my eyes closed, listening to the soft murmuring of the small waves sliding up onto the shore. I refused to think about anything but the beach and the gulf and the warm sun overhead.

But other thoughts came stealing in, one at a time. The first had to do with Mom. All those things Aunt Eva had said to me about her. Why hadn't I realized them before? Why couldn't I have figured them out by myself instead of having to have them explained to me as if I were some five-year-old? I was almost college age—almost an adult. So why wasn't I acting like one?

Well, it was definitely time I did.

And that meant seriously giving some consideration to where I was heading with my life. Not waiting to see what someone else was doing, then trying to become part of his or her existence. Mom had finally found her place. I could see now that she hadn't meant to hurt me on purpose. She'd been scared. Real people get scared. Mom was a real person. All my life I'd thought of her only as my mother. I hadn't considered that she had a right to a life that didn't have anything to do with me. And when the time came for me to go to college or to live my own life, she wasn't just supposed to sit on some shelf waiting for me to visit her at Christmas.

Which brought me back to thinking about my own life. And with that I realized I hadn't actually given an awful lot of thought to what I was going to do with it. College was little more than a year away. A year wasn't very long when I considered it. That scared me.

What would happen if I didn't go to college?

What if I ended up behind a drugstore counter, selling lipstick and cleansing cream, the same way Mom had all the years since Dad's death?

What would happen if I went to Philadelphia to live?

I'd have Mom for another year. But then what? Did I want to go to college up north?

I opened my eyes and stared out at the Gulf.

Was it true that I had made Gary a substitute for Mom in my mind? Had I been so desperately lonely that I'd latched onto him for that reason?

No, that wasn't it, I thought, my feelings for Gary were very real. I knew Gary was my first real love. And even if I never saw him again, I also knew I would always remember him that way.

Then something else Aunt Eva had said came to mind. She'd said that each of us had to find his or her own way, that we each must be true to only one person, ourself. Funny, it had sounded selfish when she'd said it. But now I was beginning to understand. After all, if someone was all mixed up and unhappy like my mom, how could she possibly be loving and giving to someone else? Even someone close to her.

By the time I stood up and began walking away from the old pier, I'd thought about myself and what I wanted to do.

I stood at the phone in the hall, my hands shaking as I punched Mom's number in Philadelphia. I heard the squeals and clicks as the call made its way up the coast, then I heard the rings; one, two, three.

"Hello?"

"Mom, it's me, Wendy."

"Wendy!" She paused. "I didn't expect you to call back so quickly." There was a nervous little laugh. "Are you calling to tell me good news?"

"Yes." I paused. "Sort of."

"I see." There was some static on the line. "I guess you'd better tell me the good news first. That way the 'sort of' news won't be so bad."

"OK. Well, I want to come up for the summer." I was rushing. "It sounds like it'll be fun. And I really want to go to The Egg Carton. OK? I mean almost as soon as I get there. You know how I love omelets."

"I know, I know." She was laughing happily.

"But, Mom—"

"Yes?"

"About school next year—" I took a deep breath, holding it until I knew my voice would be steady. "I want to come back here and stay with Aunt Eva. Mom, please, don't get it all wrong, I've really thought it over." I took another deep breath, letting it out slowly. "I think I might want to be a marine biologist, like Daddy. And the University of South Florida is one of the best places to study. Our high school has a great senior-year program that lets us work with the university people." There was more static on the line. "Mom, are you there—did you hear me?"

"Yes, yes, Wendy, I heard you." She paused. "Wendy, I'm delighted you're coming for the summer." There was another pause, a longer one. This time when she started talking again, her voice sounded funny, as if she were beginning to come down with a cold, but I knew she was crying. "And, Wendy, I'm really happy that you've decided what it is you want to do. I mean about college, and—well—I know your father would be happy, too. I know he'd be proud that you want to do the same thing he loved so much. You know we both would—"

"Mom," I said. "Mom, I love you!"

There was no answer.

"Mom?"

"Listen, Wendy!" Her voice was strong again. "Tell you what. As soon as we hang up, I'll get busy finding out about plane reservations, all that sort of thing, and send it off. You know, so you'll be able to make plans." She paused. "Oh, Wendy, I'm so glad you're coming. Oh, and I just had another thought. I'll pick up one of the menus from The Egg Carton and mail that, too." She gave a little laugh. "That way you can decide what kind of omelet you want before you get here. OK?"

"OK—great!" I answered, laughing back. But then I kind of choked. I put my hand over the receiver so she wouldn't hear that.

There was a long silence after that. Then Mom said, with a kind of nervous giggle, "I guess we'd better hang up. This call must be costing Eva a small fortune."

"Yeah," I answered with the same kind of voice. "I guess so."

"Bye, Wendy."

"Bye, Mom."

"Wendy—"I heard Mom gently clearing her throat. "I love you."

"Me, too," I said back. But I heard the click of the receiver halfway through saying it, so I wasn't sure she'd heard.

But I did love her. I really did!

Chapter Sixteen

I ran my finger gently around the top of the queen tegula, feeling the bumps and whorls but only imagining the pearly color. I had my eyes closed.

I was sitting on the carpet, leaning up against the side of my bed. The room was already getting dark. It's on the side away from the west. The Florida room would still be getting the last rays of the sun; it would be pink and orange and gold in there. I didn't feel like pink and orange and gold. I felt dark gray like my room. I was glad Aunt Eva was out shopping. If she'd been home, she'd have suggested I turn on a light, and that would have destroyed my mood. I didn't want that. The next day would be soon enough. It would be the first day back from vacation; I'd go to school and put on a happy face. I'd pretend it didn't matter to me that Gary wasn't coming back.

I knew it for certain now. Funny how all spring vacation I'd tried to convince myself not to hope that he wasn't coming back. But all the time some little part of me kept insisting I was wrong, he would be coming back to Florida.

Now I knew better. Because his father had flown early in the morning. And Gary hadn't been with him. And when I'd talked to Marlo, she'd said Gary was still in California.

I'd already decided what I was going to wear in the morning—my red cords and my white, almost-silk blouse. It was the same outfit I'd worn that first time I'd really wanted to impress Gary. One good thing, if I could call it that, the cords fit. I'd lost four pounds during the last week.

I opened my eyes and looked down at the shell in my hand. The sheen was muted in the darkening light. I told myself it would be my last look at it for a long time. Gently I put it back in its box and closed the top. In a second I'd get up and put it in my drawer. I'd put it way at the back where I wouldn't be reminded of Gary until I could stand to think of him without hurting.

The phone rang out in the hall. It sounded muffled through the closed bedroom door. It rang five times. I didn't want to answer it. It was probably Marlo wanting to know what I was going to wear to school. Well, she'd see in the morning.

It rang seven times.

That was more than Marlo usually rang.

All at once I thought of Aunt Eva. She must still be out. Maybe something was wrong. Maybe the car had broken down. I leaped up and raced for the hall.

"Hello," I said, breathing heavily into the mouthpiece.

"Hi! Wendy?"

It was Gary. Was he calling from California?

"Gary?"

"Hey, you remembered me!" he said teasingly.

"Gary?"

"Right. Hi!"

"Hi! Are you calling from California?"

"Nope. But that's where I just came from." There was a pause. "My dad came back early this morning because he had a nine o'clock meeting, but I decided to come back on a later flight. I'm at Marlo's."

"Then you're back?" It was a dumb question. What I really meant was how long was he back for? Was he going back to California? Had someone forced him to get on the plane after he'd tried to stay? And most important, why was he calling me to tell me he was back? But you can't pack all that into one sentence.

"Wendy—can we talk?"

"Aren't we?"

"Yes. No! I mean, are you doing something you can stop for a while? What I mean is, can I come over and talk to you in person? Now? Or

148

soon? Listen, I really did just get in. My suitcase is sitting right here by the phone. I thought about a lot of stuff on the plane. Stuff I want to tell you. And I think I'd better talk about it before I lose my nerve. Do you understand?"

My mind raced back to the last time he'd wanted me to understand, when he'd given me the shell. I was sure I'd understood then. "I think so," I said, trying to keep the unhappiness out of my voice.

"Good. Then can I come over?"

I remembered Aunt Eva coming home from shopping. "Maybe I'd better meet you someplace. How about down at the end of the path? You know where I mean?" I'd almost said, "Remember, it's where we first met?"

"Sure. Twenty minutes, OK?"

"OK." I hung up quickly, before I could change my mind, before he could say something else that might change it for me.

Everything was golden. Only the edge of a huge Sunkist sun sat on the top of the waves. Gary was standing by the end of the path. He was golden, too. His face, his hair, the shirt he was wearing, the rolled-up, dress slacks he must've worn on the plane, they were all golden.

"Hi!" I said, smiling.

"Hi!" he said back and reached for my hand. We walked down toward the dark path of wet sand that edged the water, then along it.

"Wendy," he said, after we'd walked in silence for several minutes, "what I want to talk about—well, it's really kind of hard for me to say. Because I really like you a lot. I mean I knew that I liked you before I went back to California. As a friend—a really good friend."

A friend!

"Do you understand?"

I nodded, although I didn't understand at all.

He shook his head and dropped my hand. "No, I think I'm explaining this all wrong. Let me start at the beginning."

We were still walking. Only he was a little apart from me now. Somewhere inside I realized we were walking toward the old wooden pier.

"There's this girl in California. Cynthia. We went out together for a really long time. Then, just before I was going to move, we broke up. But then we got back together again, and I was mad about having to move. I wanted to stay in California so we could be together." He stopped talking suddenly. He shoved his hands into his pockets, then took them out again. "I was so mad that I'd pretty much decided to do something when I went out there this last week with my Dad."

I nodded, listening. I didn't ask why he'd returned to Florida.

"I spent the whole week with my friends. There was a party Cynthia and I went to. We all had pizza together. I had dinner at her parents' house. They're really nice people. It was a great week; I had a good time. It was just like when I lived there before." He paused.

I nodded again, somehow feeling sorry.

"And I kissed Cynthia."

We'd reached the pier at the same time that he'd said that. I turned away. I couldn't believe he'd actually told me that. Why? I could have handled the rest, eventually. But why tell me that? I stared at the pier, now mostly a dark, broken shadow in the final glow of the afternoon. My eyes felt hot, and they hurt. I hurt other places, too. I hurt in my heart. *Do hearts actually break?* I wondered.

"Wendy? Are you listening?"

I turned back to face him. A sudden feeling of having lived through this before slid over me. He was just as I'd seen him that night of the party. His good slacks rolled up, hands on his hips, looking miserable because he was thinking of the girl he loved. So I was supposed to be the good friend he could talk to about her! Such a good friend that he felt he could lay all his romantic problems on me and I'd help him find a way to keep his girl. Well, forget it! There's only so much one person can take. "I think I've listened long enough," I said. "I'm sorry, Gary. But I think you'll just have to work out your own problems—without my help!" I turned away quickly.

But he was quick. He reached out and grabbed my arm. "Wendy, whoa!"

I pulled against him.

"Wendy—wait! Darn it, will you listen! I warned you I was bad at explaining things."

"Oh, you explain very well!"I glared at him.

"No." He shook his head. "You didn't let me finish." He was still holding my arm. "If I let go of you, will you let me do just that?"

"Yes," I said, lying.

He let go.

"Good-bye, Gary!" I shot at him and started off again.

He grabbed me, this time holding both shoulders. "I should've known better," he muttered. "Now you listen this time." He shook me slightly. "Wendy, look at me!"

I did. I could feel the warmth of his breath on my face.

"Now, as I said, I kissed Cynthia." He paused. "And when I did, I realized I wasn't really in love with her. What's more, I realized I wasn't sure I ever had been. I don't know. Maybe it was some kind of infatuation. She *is* pretty." His hands squeezed on my shoulders. "But the important thing to me was that I realized Cynthia and I had never been friends. And that *is* important. How can you possibly love someone without being friends first?" He stopped as if he were expecting an answer from me.

But all I could do was to stare back at him, aware of how close he was to me, of his strong hands holding my shoulders, and of the rise and fall of his chest as he breathed.

"Don't you see what I'm trying to say, Wendy? You and I are friends. Good friends. And I think we have the kind of friendship that can, at least I hope so, build into something really important."

"Oh," I said softly and realized that I'd been holding my breath almost since he'd grabbed my shoulders.

"Now, if I let go," he asked in a low voice, "will you try and run away again?"

"I won't," I promised, telling the truth.

His hands let go of my shoulders and moved gently down my arms to my waist. Then he pulled me close. When his lips met mine, I knew for sure that we weren't just friends any longer.

We hope you enjoyed reading this book. There are many other Sweet Dreams titles available. Ask for them in your local bookshop or newsagent. Two new titles are published each month.

If you would like to know more about Sweet Dreams, or if you have difficulty obtaining any of the books locally, or if you would like to tell us what you think of the series, write to:—

<u>United Kingdom</u>
Kim Prior,
Corgi Books,
Century House,
61-63 Uxbridge Road,
London W5 5SA,
England

<u>Australia</u>
Sally Porter,
Corgi and
Bantam Books,
26 Harley Crescent,
Condell Park 220,
N.S.W., Australia